The Priestess Chronicles
Volume 2

Relic

Seeker

Books by Fiona Tarr

Covenant of Grace Series

Destiny of Kings

Seed of Hope

Legacy of Power

Heir of Vengeance

The Ehud Dagger – Novella

The Eternal Realm

The Jericho Prophecy

Delilah and the Dark God

Reign of Retribution

The Priestess Chronicles

Call of the Druids

Relic Seeker

Chapter 1

Will you tell me where we are going this time Raziel? Ariela spoke the words in her mind as the swirling debris rose from the ground of the village she was leaving behind. There was no reply, but she didn't expect one. The Angel had already sent her into the future, with no knowledge, no expectation and most of all, no clear idea of what she needed to do.

So much had changed since she left the past behind. She now understood there would be no returning to her family; they were lost to her past and there seemed to be only the ability to move forward in time, not back.

She felt her body become weightless and held tightly to the warmth of Culaan and Genevieve's hand. Her stomach lurched a little, but the feeling was fleeting as she took a deep breath and relaxed knowing now what to expect from the time shift. Leaves continued to brush her face, as sand grazed her cheeks. Ariela smiled knowing that her new friends would be joining her this time. Travelling through time, doing the Angel's bidding, wouldn't be as lonely anymore.

Now, she was courageous enough to open her eyes to the Holy realm she had only seen in visions the last time she passed the threshold of time. The golden light was brilliant and Ariela could see nothing clearly. Figures moved, unrecognisable in the brightness that surrounded her.

She could still feel Genevieve and Culaan's hands in hers, but they were nowhere in sight. The world around her was dazzling and shining like white gold and the sense of peace seeped into her soul. Her hair streamed out behind her like ribbons on the breeze and even though she knew she had no need to draw breath in this place, her chest rose and fell rhythmically.

Before she could fully absorb the scene before her, the light blurred into unrecognisable streaks of lightning and she closed her eyes to avoid the nausea rising up in her stomach.

As she waited to find where Raziel would take them, she reached out with her spirit for her friends, and fought a sense of panic as she realised she could no longer feel their hands in hers or sense their presence.

****

Culaan felt Ariela's hand slip from his as the sensation of spinning abated. He opened his eyes with panicked urgency and looked around into the gloomy forest.

'Did you hear what Morrigan said?' Genevieve asked Culaan casually as she tried to focus on his face in the dim light of predawn grey that greeted them.

'Where is Ariela?' Culaan turned around more than once, his eyes squinting into the dim surroundings trying to make out where they were, where Ariela was.

Genevieve lifted her bow from her shoulder and the ethereal light sprang into a bright silvery glow. Culaan pulled his sword from its scabbard and it too lit the early morning dimness with mystical light. The two warriors circled defensively with their backs together.

'She isn't here Cul.' Genevieve could sense her best friend's panic through his body which shuddered with supressed fear and anger.

'That damned Angel has taken her and left us behind.' Culaan snarled the words and Genevieve felt her own anxiety rising.

'No, we are not in the land of our clans Culaan. Look!' Genevieve nodded to the flat plain that greeted them beyond the trees. 'She must be here somewhere.'

Just as the pair of warriors relaxed, the sound of movement amongst the thick forest caused Genevieve to redraw her bow.

'Don't make any sudden moves.' Culaan warned.

'Since when have I needed your instruction in battle!'

Culaan looked over his shoulder and caught sight of their foe. 'We are surrounded. What was that damned Angel thinking?' He moved his sword between himself and the closest warrior. It seemed to buzz and sizzle with his frustration.

Genevieve released an arrow that flew through the air, pinning the collar of the closest warrior's fur-lined coat to the tree branch just behind his left ear. 'The next one goes between your eyes.' The arrow sparkled with light but didn't ignite the coat or the branch. 'I'm getting the hang of this.' The Huntress congratulated herself.

'And that wasn't a sudden movement now was it!' Culaan growled as he rolled his sword around his wrist, the lightning like effect leaving streaks in the pre-dawn light.

'It be the son of Oden Atta.' A young man's voice rang out as the first rays of sun crested the distant mountains.

'Don't you be going any closer Blaze.' A broad-shouldered man moved forward, pushing the boy behind him protectively.

'Look at him Atta. I'm sure it's him. Look at that sword!' The boy peered around the warrior to get a better look as he bounced from foot to foot with obvious excitement.

'Is the boy right? Are you sent from the gods?'

Culaan looked at Genevieve and smiled. The Huntress returned the grin mischievously and shrugged.

'Technically, yes.' Culaan answered carefully, wiping the grin from his face as he cautiously sheathed his sword, the light disappearing instantly.

'What happens in the after-life for those who impersonate gods?' Genevieve whispered. Culaan frowned appearing to suddenly reconsider the wisdom of his deceit.

'See Atta. I told you he's Thor. Just look at him and she must be Skathi.'

'Take a breath Blaze. We'll see. Skathi or not, will you lower that bow woman?'

Genevieve released the notched arrow from the bow-string and the weapon immediately lost a little of its potency as the mystical light extinguished. The Huntress returned the arrow to the quiver on her back and shouldered her weapon. Her left hand remained close to the short-bladed sword strapped to her thigh and the newcomer allowed his eyes to wander down her long curvaceous leg. He smiled as he saw her thumb the hilt of her weapon and returned his gaze to her eyes.

'My name is Reznor. This is my lad Blaze. He seems to think you two might be the answer to his prayers.' The big man moved forward in greeting, his shoulders unnaturally wide with the thick fur coat he wore, but there was something about his manner that held unspoken power.

'Why have you been praying little man?' Genevieve missed the boy's scowl as she watched Reznor, admiring his strong stature. The rising sun sparkled in his ice-blue eyes and when he grinned, she returned the gesture in spite of herself.

'We have the worst kind of enemy at our door. The kind that undermines our culture and faith, but we can't vanquish them in any traditional fight. They are too powerful for that.' Reznor addressed the question.

'An old and common story. We have come from just such a battle.' Culaan moved between Reznor and Genevieve breaking their eye contact. 'What makes your cause noble enough to warrant help from the gods?'

'Not noble. We only seek freedom from the yoke of others.'

'It's the nature of strong men to rule. Who is this master you seek freedom from?'

'The Roman Empire of course!' Reznor frowned his confusion. Shouldn't gods who have come to aid them know who their enemies are?

The mere mention of the Romans raised Culaan's heckles and he growled his response. 'Now that is a vermin worth calling on the divine for. When do we start?'

Chapter 2

'How in Heaven's name do you manage to dress me in the middle of a time shift?' Ariela knew Raziel was not about to answer her questions, but she felt an overwhelming need to vent her frustration. Culaan and Genevieve were nowhere in sight and she was dressed in a short tunic worn by slaves. Gone was the clothing she wore when she left Morrigan behind.

The steam rose from her lips as she breathed and the early morning chill was seeping into her bones. Her toes were growing numb in the damp dew-covered grass. She would have done almost anything to have her hooded robe right now.

'There you are. Hurry up child. You are late enough already.' A heavy-set woman with a long, thick plait and wide hips grabbed Ariela by the arm and pulled her roughly down a stone path and into an alleyway. Ariela knew better than to protest. The woman was dressed in a fine robe of linen drawn at the waist by a silver and turquoise sash and spoke with obvious authority.

The Priestess waited, knowing that it would take time to understand where she was and what the Angel wanted her to do. Last time was no different. At least this time she didn't wake up in a dark, damp alley and immediately get attacked by a soldier. At least this time she hadn't had to kill anyone, not yet anyway.

'The Master will expect you to be more punctual in the future. You can cook?' The woman blurted out instructions, looking back at Ariela for confirmation as she rushed them through a low stone doorway and into a hot cookhouse barely ten paces wide.

'Cook?' Ariela stumbled over the rough stone floor. She couldn't remember ever having been required to cook in her life. Even as a Priestess her duties had never included cooking duty. She was the daughter of a High Priestess after all and spent most of her time training with her father in the use of weapons, not cooking knives.

'Oh never mind. You will learn.' The woman impatiently pushed Ariela ahead of her, past the hearth and into an open storeroom full of produce. 'There is a sack of potatoes over there.' The woman pointed, the folds of skin hanging loosely below her sleeveless robe. 'The others will be here any minute. You can get started peeling and cutting potatoes while I go and see to the Master of the house.'

Ariela stared at the hessian bag at her feet as the woman hurried away. *Where on earth was she? More to the point, in what time was she and who was that woman?* She considered the architecture that surrounded the alleyway she had been dragged through and the ornate stone archway that marked the entrance to the cookhouse. None of it looked familiar. The stonework was almost translucent white and carved with intricate patterns. Even the flagstones on the floor were made of foreign material.

The young Priestess sighed, pushing her concerns aside. At least the cookhouse wasn't cold. How they were going to fit more people in such a small space confused her, but she had other things to worry about. Where were Culaan and Genevieve? She felt lost, even more so than she did the last time Raziel landed her in a foreign land.

'Who are you?' A young woman with dark brown eyes and plump cheeks stood frowning suspiciously at Ariela as she moved out of the storeroom with an arm full of potatoes. The Priestess juggled them unsuccessfully in surprise.

'I, I'm new. My name is Ariela,' she said as she bent down to collect her lost cargo.

'Oh!' The girl knelt to help. 'Ariela? You're not from around here then!' The girl eyed the Priestess curiously.

'How can you tell?' Ariela wiped the sweat from her palms, suddenly feeling nervous. She knew Raziel would have made her able to speak and understand the local language, but what could have raised the girl's suspicions?

'Your name is pretty foreign.' The girl smiled spontaneously, her rounded cheeks framed in welcoming dimples. 'Are you really supposed to be here?'

Ariela could only nod. 'Well before the Mistress returns, you had better reconsider your name.' Ariela's eyes grew wider. Was this girl about to expose her? 'Try Alexandria. It's more believable.'

The girl smiled again and turned her back on Ariela, taking a handful of potatoes with her. She placed them on the wooden table in the centre of the cookhouse and turned to looked over her shoulder. 'Well, you had best get started before the Mistress returns,' and she began effortlessly peeling the potatoes with a small knife; peel and blade flashing faster than the Priestess could focus.

Ariela fumbled with her bundle and joined the girl, her mind racing with questions. Her mouth opened and closed as she tried unsuccessfully to put words into sentences.

Finally, she gave up and joined her new-found ally in preparing the food.

****

Ariela's hands were red and covered in small cuts by the time the preparation was done. The Priestess looked at her palms and shook her head. She had trained for years with sword and bow. She had calloused strong fingers, lean muscles and was extremely fit. How was it then that she was so useless with a peeling knife?

'Alexandria, if you are finished, the Senator needs his office tidied and the staircase needs dusting.' The Mistress, who Ariela now knew as Katerina—not that she was allowed to use her real name—called through the entrance from the cookhouse to the main dining room.

'Coming Mistress.' Ariela wiped her hands on her apron and untied it quickly.

'Don't worry, you'll get used to it soon enough. There is no rest to be had here until the sun sets.' The girl's dimples returned. They had chatted quietly while

they worked and Ariela now knew quite a lot about her
new friend. Ophelia seemed to have her finger on the
pulse of the entire Estate and if anyone was going to be
able to help Ariela work out why she was here, it would
be this young, plump, vivacious woman.

Chapter 3

Culaan entered the camp of their new-found friends. Anyone fighting the tyranny of the Roman Empire was to be considered an ally as far as he was concerned. Yet part of him wanted to leave these people and do whatever he needed to do to find Ariela, but he knew that the Angel would look out for her and he felt somehow drawn to these people.

Genevieve and Culaan walked behind Reznor and his son, a small group of warriors trailing along behind. The warrior who nearly lost his ear to Genevieve seemed to be watching her intently, but Culaan couldn't blame him for that.

A woman with a pan full of hot water gaped at the newcomers and nudged her friend, who looked over her shoulder; the same stunned look growing across her features.

'Anyone would think they had seen a ghost.' Genevieve lent close to Culaan's ear so as not to be overheard. Culaan answered with a frown and a shrug.

'Some refreshment.' Reznor ordered to no-one in particular. A flurry of activity exploded from the stillness as people suddenly realised they had all stopped what they were doing and scrambled to look busy.

Reznor turned to Culaan and Genevieve and smiled. 'It works every time. We don't get visitors all that often, unless they are Roman Centurions coming to order us about.'

'Why do they order you about?' Culaan accepted the cup of water passed to him by a petite girl with dark hair and even darker eyes. He hesitated a moment, trying to reconcile her appearance with the rest of the village who had blonde or red hair not unlike his own. 'Thank you.' He added clumsily to the young woman who smiled in reply.

'Five seconds without Ariela and already you are flirting.' Genevieve teased.

'Don't get started Genie. I was just being polite and now you've gone and reminded me that I should be out looking for her.'

'You brought others?' Reznor raised an eyebrow.

'That's a long story. I'll tell you about it when the time is right. Why do the Romans order you about?'

'We try and live a peaceful life. We grow crops and raise livestock, but they see our size and our strength and they want to control us. We fight in their wars, for gold and they order us about as if we are their slaves.'

Culaan considered the Roman Empire had grown even stronger since what was only his yesterday. He wanted to ask what year it was but that would have raised even more questions. 'Who rules in Rome?'

The question seemed odd to the warrior but since gods didn't likely concern themselves with worldly governments, Reznor brushed off his curiosity. 'We have two Emperors in reality. Constantine The Second rules in Rome while he leaves the north to his brother-in-law Licinius. They have a treaty of sorts, but I doubt it will last long. There is no love between them.'

'How is it you think to gain your freedom?' Culaan knew nothing of the gods these people followed. He understood a little about Druid magic. He understood his own land, but this foreign place was making him uncomfortable. He realised he was not enlightened with the discovery of the Emperor. He still had no idea where in the Roman Empire he was or who these people were.

'Well if you had asked that question yesterday, I would have said I had no idea. We've been doing the Romans' bidding for generations. But I think if they come to force us to fight again, we'll just push you out front and you can strike them down with that lightning bolt of a sword or *she* can shoot them with brilliant flaming arrows and they will know the gods are on our side.' There was no missing the sarcasm and when Reznor patted Culaan on the shoulder, both men laughed.

Culaan had the sneaking suspicion that Reznor wasn't fooled by a few brilliantly shining weapons, even if his boy was.

'Welcome.' A woman's voice almost made Culaan jump. It was as though she had appeared from thin air and the hairs on the back of his neck tingled with the surprise.

'This is Andronica, our village Healer for want of a better word.' Reznor offered almost apologetically.

'A pleasure to meet you.' Culaan watched the woman as her eyes seemed to pierce into his very soul. He knew Genevieve felt the discomfort too, he had seen her stiffen at the sound of the woman's voice.

'Reznor, you seem to always bring home all the strays.' Culaan recognised the insincerity in Andronica's tone but Reznor seemed undisturbed by her manner.

Andronica turned and walked away without further comment and Culaan found he couldn't take his eyes from her retreating back. She was tall and lean, with golden red hair like his own.

He wasn't attracted to her but he was confused by his feelings, so much so that he looked to Genie to help him clarify he wasn't imagining it. She raised her eyebrow and twisted her lip in a way that made it clear that the woman unnerved her too.

Reznor seemed to sense their feelings. 'I apologise for Andronica. She isn't one of us. In fact, no one really knows where she came from. She too was a *stray*, but her skills at healing can't be argued with. Come, let us share a meal and I can tell you of our woes.'

'You lead these people then?' Culaan assumed he did, but he wanted to be sure. He followed Reznor toward a large hall made of cut logs, bound together with clay. The building reminded Culaan of home and for just a moment he wondered if leaving his clan had been the right choice. *Where is Ariela? He'd only come for her and she was gone, nowhere in sight.* Culaan hoped again that she was alright.

****

Andronica's skin was crawling. The feeling had filled her with dread since dawn and at first, she had thought the two newcomers to the village were the cause, but now that she had been close to both of them, she wasn't so sure.

There was something about them though. They seemed familiar somehow but they were not the major source of her magic stirring, she was sure of it. There was someone else out there capable of power, great power and she had to find them before they ruined her plans.

Andronica closed the heavy door on her cottage and moved quickly to her bed. She pushed her feather filled mattress aside and found the latch to the small door in the bed's wooden base. She peered into the darkness for a moment before pushing her hand in and feeling around for what she needed.

As she pulled out the heavy metal amulet with a green stone in the centre, she felt a sudden sense of ease. The star-shape was surrounded by a wide circle and the prized possession tingled at her touch, bringing a smile to her lips.

She placed it around her neck and settled it underneath her tunic, low over her cleavage. It felt warm as it touched her skin, but there was also an icy sharp jab that reassured her the amulet still possessed the power she needed.

Chapter 4

Ariela climbed the staircase to the Senator's office. She touched the white stone balustrade and marvelled at how shiny and smooth the surface was. The pale grey veins of colour that ran through the stone were beautiful and like nothing the Priestess had ever seen before.

As she reached the top, she stopped. Katerina had told her the office was at the far end of the passageway. Ariela made her way down the hall, past the heavy wooden doors lining each side. They were closed shut, holding the mystery of their contents from sight.

Ariela reached the end of the long hall and knocked on the Senator's door. She waited for a reply and when none came, she carefully opened the door to enter. The room was vast. The walls were lined with floor-to-ceiling shelves filled to overflowing with scrolls and manuscripts, maps and even some rare bound books.

'Why am I here Raziel?' The Priestess wondered out aloud, but instead of stopping to await the answer she knew wouldn't come, she started cleaning the Senator's office. The wooden desk was covered in papers, so Ariela decided to start with the shelves.

There were stone pedestals with various statues placed evenly in each corner of the room. They collected dust easily and the Priestess worked hard to remove all the dirt. She opened the window and flicked the dust from her rag, deciding to leave the window ajar to air out the smell of stale wine and tobacco.

She was so focussed on her work that she failed to hear the young man approach but she felt his eyes on her back as he stood with his shoulder leaning against the shelving, an amused smile on his face.

'A new girl. Nice.'

Ariela wasn't sure if she should ignore the man or respond. Was it rude to answer him or rude not to?

'Yes sir.' She answered cautiously.

The man moved forward. Ariela studied him, trying to decide who he was. She judged him to be a few years older than her. He was clean-shaven with dark eyes and a hooked nose, not unlike the beak of an eagle. There was nothing attractive about him. The smile he wore failed to reach his eyes and seemed somehow forced. He didn't walk like a warrior, but Ariela remained wary and tried to maintain her distance.

'Katerina makes lovely choices in staff you know.' Ariela only nodded and moved away to continue her work but the man reached out and took her by the wrist, her cleaning rag hanging limply in her hand as he pulled her to him.

'I have to finish cleaning the Senator's office.' Ariela struggled to distract the man.

'My name is Constantius The Second, son of the Emperor of Rome. Rest assured the Senator will have no issue with you dallying with me instead of finishing the dusting.'

Ariela suddenly realised her choices were limited. She couldn't just kill this man who was attacking her like she did in Galatia. She stopped struggling and smiled at the man before her and dropped her eyes, bowing her head submissively.

'An honour to meet you Sir.' She followed with a curtsy and then batted her eyelashes just slightly. She racked her brain for a way to make him release her wrist, which he now seemed to be holding even more tightly. His whole body was growing rigid with tension and she suddenly felt scared.

She closed her eyes and allowed her power to surge forward for just a split second. The sensation was like the release of energy from the air after a thunder storm and Constantius yelped as he let go of her wrist.

'What is the name of Heaven was that?' Constantius rubbed his hand and arm as though he had been burnt. Ariela had felt nothing from the jolt. Absorbing her own energy was always like that.

'Whatever do you mean Sir?' She feigned innocence and took the opportunity to leave the room but she was too slow. The Emperor's son reached out and grabbed her again. This time Ariela allowed a little scorn to cross her face and Constantius seemed to respond. He let go of Ariela slowly, studying her face as though suddenly reconsidering his options.

'I just wanted to show you something before you left.' His tone was suddenly apologetic. 'It's the Senator's for now, but I've petitioned my father to let me take it to

Rome.' He moved across the room and opened a door on the shelving between the two windows that were located at the front of the building.

'Come, I want you to see this.'

Ariela eyed him suspiciously but her curiosity was piqued now and she felt Constantius understood that the jolt of energy was something she could control. She was wary as she approached the now open cupboard. A feeling of increased energy surged as she came closer. She could feel the hair on her arms rising and there was a fluttering of butterflies in her stomach.

'Isn't it amazing?' Constantius's expression was hard to read. He seemed as though he were trying to impress the new girl and Ariela suddenly felt sorry for him. She knew what it was like to be Royal. Her Uncle had tried to marry her off to a prince as a trophy of war, a barter for peace. She understood his plight; his lack of identity.

Ariela peered into the cupboard and gasped. 'What is it?' The golden circle of metal was intricately carved in a language Ariela had never seen before. The symbols were finely inscribed but they were bold in nature and seemed to carry purpose and power.

The Priestess could feel the magical power coming from the circlet and the closer she came to it, the more it spoke to her.

'No one knows really. But isn't it beautiful? I don't know why I'm showing this to you really. No one is supposed to know it's here.'

Ariela suddenly felt uncomfortable. Was this Raziel's doing? 'Then you had best pack it away. *You* might not get into trouble but I certainly will.'

Constantius reached out and touched Ariela's cheek delicately. His demeanour totally the opposite from before. 'You are very beautiful.'

'And you are very nice Sir, but please, close the cupboard and let me finish my work before anyone discovers me not working.'

Constantius pushed the cupboard closed. It was as though a flame was extinguished with the door closing. The Emperor's son's eyes lit up as soon as the door closed and he turned to Ariela who now stood right next to him. He grabbed her by the waist and pushed her into the shelving. Scrolls dropped to the floor with the force and Ariela gasped in surprise.

Constantius kissed her hard on the lips and pushed his body firmly into her. Ariela had no control of her power. The attack happened so quickly and the burst of energy she released was unregulated.

The last thing she saw as she ran from the room was blood trickling from Constantius's nose and his unconscious, limp body positioned unnaturally against the far wall of the office.

Chapter 5

'I should have warned you about him.' Ophelia was calm as Ariela blurted out what had happened in the Senator's office. 'He is crazy that one.' Ophelia circled her finger by her temple and crossed her eyes at the Priestess who laughed despite her racing heart.

'He'll have me put to death or at the very least, thrown out on the street.'

'Nah!' Ophelia waved her hand in the air and then carried on calmly preparing food for the evening meal. 'He probably won't even remember. I told you, he is crazy. He really isn't all there. One second he is violent the next he is your best friend and then he is off with the fairies in a trance someplace else. Why do you think the Emperor's son is all the way out here in remote territory with a minor Senator and the Goth mercenary tribes?'

'Goth mercenary tribes?' Constantius was suddenly forgotten as Ariela thought about Culaan and Genevieve.

'Yep. This area is full of them. Look, I know you are not from around here. I know more than you realise, but you really need to stop asking stupid questions like that in case someone who doesn't turn a blind eye like me, notices.'

Ariela frowned, suddenly curious about Ophelia. 'Why *do* you turn a blind eye?'

Ophelia shrugged and Ariela reached out with her talent. The girl turned on her then and slapped her. The Priestess gasped in surprise and took a few steps back. She drew on her energy ready to defend herself but Ophelia just put her hand in the air palm out. 'Don't even think about it. I know you're powerful, powerful enough to turn me to vapour definitely, but you are not the only magic wielder here and believe me, you don't want to be discovered just yet. Mind you, I'd be surprised if she doesn't already know you are here and that little display upstairs with Constantius, well that will have confirmed her suspicions.'

Ariela had sat back on the wooden bench, her mouth open and her eyes wide. 'Who are you?'

'Well I could ask you the same question you know.' Ophelia smiled sweetly. There was no sting in her words.

'I had no choice, well I did, but I didn't. He attacked me in such a rush I had no time to collect my thoughts. It was purely a defensive strike.'

'I believe you. Are you new to your powers?' Ophelia carried on chopping vegetables and threw a carrot at Ariela who didn't miss the hint.

She left the bench and joined her new friend. 'I'm not so much new to them, but new to using them to their full extent and they are evolving.'

'Hmmm.' Ophelia carried on with her work. She handed more vegetables to Ariela and then collected up a large piece of lamb. As she chopped the joints apart, she seemed to be considering something, gazing at Ariela between downward swings of a heavy meat clever.

'Look, my powers are limited. I'm just a minder of sorts. I could sense your magic the moment you arrived, but I had to be careful. You could have been as much of a threat as she is.'

'Who is she?' Ariela raised an eyebrow at Ophelia's silence.

'Let me ask a few questions first.' Ariela nodded. 'You are not from around here, so where are you from?'

'That is difficult to answer. I'm from Israel originally, but my last stop was east of here in a place called Galatia, but it's hard because it might not be called Galatia anymore.' Ariela waited for the concept to sink in and Ophelia nodded slowly as she started to grasp what was going on.

'I need an ally here. I'm not used to being a servant.'

'No! Really!' Ophelia didn't hide the sarcasm from her voice.

'Well I *am* the daughter of the King's sister and a Priestess of the Order of Shiloh. I have a genuine defence you know.'

'Royal then!' Ophelia smiled.

'I'm sorry. I don't know the customs, the people, heck I don't even know the year.'

Ophelia laughed. 'You realise how insane that sounds don't you? I might have to take you and put you with our crazy friend upstairs.'

'That reminds me, have you heard if he is alright?' Ariela was genuinely curious. She didn't want to hurt him. He just hadn't given her much of a choice.

'He is fine. Some bumps and bruises. He'll be unconscious all afternoon.'

'What did you tell Katerina?'

'The truth. That he tried to have his way with you and that you pushed him away and he struck his head on the statue.'

'And she believed you and she isn't going to throw me out?'

'He won't remember and if he does, I told you, he is loopy. No one will believe that a little girl like you could throw him across the room and everyone knows he has a soft spot for pretty girls. Why do you think we had an opening to bring you on?'

The thought of the Emperor's son accosting other servants left a bad taste in the Priestess's mouth, but she suddenly remembered something important. 'Do you know what he showed me?' Ariela asked quietly, looking over her shoulder to make sure no one could hear.

Ophelia laughed. 'The same thing he shows all the girls I expect.'

Ariela blushed. 'No, not that. He didn't get that far thank goodness.' The Priestess smiled at her own embarrassment. 'He showed me something in a locked cupboard. He was very proud of it and I could feel it had power.'

'What did it look like?' Ophelia actually stopped chopping meat and lent in closer to listen.

'It was golden. A circle with a locking clip that seemed to spring open. It had engravings all over it, in a language I don't know.'

'Draw the symbols for me?' Ophelia insisted. 'Just with your finger on the bench here.' The young woman tapped the counter with her hand. 'Can you recall any of them?'

Ariela closed her eyes and tried to imagine them. 'Everything was very angular, like this.' She drew a straight line from the bottom of the bench to the right, then up to the top centre, then down to the left and then all the way back to the bottom crossing over the first line and ending level with it on the other side. The symbol was like a diamond with long legs and Ophelia mumbled quietly to herself.

'It's Goth. They don't use it much anymore. They nearly all write in the Roman symbols now. Where did you say this circlet was?'

'In a locked cupboard in the Senator's office, concealed amongst the ornaments on the main shelves, between the two front windows. Constantius said he was petitioning his father to let him have it and take it to Rome.'

'Oh no. That can't happen. If it is what I think it is we either need to bury it, destroy it or use it ourselves.'

'What do you think it is?'

'Brísingamen. I'm sure of it.'

'What on earth is Brísingamen? I've never heard of it.'

'It's an ancient Goth relic. It is said to be the necklace worn by the goddess Freya.'

'How did it find its way here?'

'I am guessing the Romans stole it from a Goth tribesman. The legend says it has magical powers and can be used by a wielder with magical strength not unlike your own. It is thought to be able to do two things—bind someone's magic forever or, move the wearer back through time.'

Ariela raised her eyebrows and placed her hand over her mouth to stifle her gasp. 'I could go back home with it!'

'You could, but moving back through time has huge negative consequences. Just the slightest change to the past will rewrite the future. But it explains why *She's* here.'

'She? Who is She and why does it explain why She's here?'

'We don't really know who *She* is yet. I belong to a group called the Guardians. We sort of keep an eye on the world of magic and in particular, powerful wielders and relics that those strong with magic like you use to amplify their gift.'

'I'm having a little trouble understanding this. Sorry. I come from a time when magic is forbidden.' Ariela wrung her hands unconsciously.

'That's nothing new. Governments, Kings and Religions have been forbidding magic for eons and for good reason. Not everyone with power uses it for good, in fact most people with the kind of power you have definitely don't use it for good even when they think they are.'

'I didn't even realise there were many of us who could wield the kind of power I've been given. Isn't all power given by God? If people misuse it why doesn't He just take it away?'

Ophelia laughed again. This time there was no humour in it. 'That is so sweet and utterly naïve. Seriously! Even if I believed in a single god, if what you say is true then there would be no evil power and the Guardians would never have been needed. No, there are people out there born with or who acquire great power and they use it for all the wrong reasons and no one, no god has ever stopped them as far as I have seen.'

Ariela suddenly looked at Ophelia and saw her for the first time. She was young but there was something wizened about her — the confidence or maybe the way she held herself.

'So, what does *She* want?'

'She has been traveling as you have, through time. We believe She acquires a relic of power from each time-line and we are yet to understand exactly what She hopes to do. If she is chasing Brísingamen, and that seems very likely, then she either wants to bind someone or she wants it for herself. At this moment, my role is to ensure she never finds it.'

'Do you have help?' Ariela asked hoping there were more Ophelia's around to aid them.

'Yes.' Ophelia smiled.

'Who?'

'You of course.' Both girls laughed and then Ariela stopped suddenly remembering Culaan and Genevieve.

'I came with friends. I just need to find where they are. I can only hope that they are alright.'

Chapter 6

'No shiny swords or bows now. That would be cheating. Let's put strength against strength.'

'But I'm a god you say. Wouldn't I have god-like strength?' Culaan smiled at Reznor's sudden confusion. His face showed he was still undecided about the two newcomers.

'You win, we go find where your girl is at. I win, you stay and help us against the Romans.' Reznor held out his hand for an agreement.

'That implies I can't go and find my friend on my own. You're not maintaining we are prisoners here, are you Reznor?' Culaan swung his sword menacingly and Genevieve smiled from the side lines.

'Of course not. This is just for amusement. You can't have a fight without something to bet on.' Reznor stretched his arms behind his back and drew his own weapon.

'Why do you get to have all the fun Culaan?' Genevieve had seen enough. 'I want to join in the competition.'

'Girls don't fight.' A tall young warrior stepped forward smiling. Culaan recognised him from the forest.

He knew he was goading Genevieve and she rose to the challenge.

'Well I'm no ordinary girl, so you can make an exception. How's your ear by the way?' It seemed Genevieve recognised him too.

'I can tell you're far from ordinary. My ear is just fine by the way. You missed.' The warrior continued to grin and Genevieve grew more agitated.

'I missed on purpose. Be careful or I'll wipe that grin from your pretty little face, boy.' The warrior didn't take offence as the Huntress intended, instead he rubbed his hand on his tunic and drew his sword.

'My name is Griffin. My friends call me Griff.'

'Griffin it is then.' Genevieve grinned as the young man finally scowled at her.

'Ignore her Griff, she is just trying to rile you.' Reznor warned, suddenly realising the girl was seasoned. He eyed her and she read his gaze, nodding she wouldn't seriously hurt the young man.

She laughed at herself. He was probably the same age as her but somehow, after travelling through time she felt as old as the years that had been taken away from her.

Griffin's hips were thin, his shoulders broad and strong, his eyes young and inviting. She shook her mind back to the looming fight and drew her sword. It wasn't her weapon of choice but she was skilled enough with it.

Genevieve grinned mockingly at Griffin who took the bait easily. He lunged forward with his heavy sword which took too long to bring to bear. Genevieve stepped aside and slapped him on the backside with the flat of her blade.

'Play nice!' Culaan warned, refraining from using her name, not wanting to dissuade the illusion of their godly powers just yet.

Genevieve's grin only grew wider as she stepped back to await Griffin's next attack. All eyes were on the pair now. The fight between Reznor and Culaan had been forgotten for now.

Griffin circled more warily, taking the time to gauge his opponent with a little more respect. Griffin moved forward, but feigned a lunge to the left and swayed to the right, coming around Genevieve's side but the Huntress was quick and easily blocked his lunge with her short sword. The ring of steel on steel rang out around the village as both blades caught each other repeatedly.

Griffin stood confidently now, but his heavy sword was beginning to feel like a bag of rocks and even his young, strong body was slowly giving out on him. Genevieve sensed the moment she had been waiting for.

'You men always overcompensate with those big swords.' She giggled at the scowl Griffin offered. 'They really have no place in close combat or long battles.'

'They can cleave a man's head clean off his shoulders.' Griffin protested.

'Lucky I'm not a man then.' Genevieve stepped in as Griffin brought his sword to bear but instead of meeting it with her weapon, she moved to his left, away from the initial arc of the sword, tossed her blade to her left hand and took Griffin in the jaw with a right uppercut.

She shook her hand in the air and cringed at the pain, but smiled as she watched Griffin's eyes roll back in his head and his body slump to the ground like a rag doll.

The crowd of villagers who had gathered to see the training bouts all moaned and gasped as their young hero hit the ground, blood and saliva dripping from his mouth.

'He fought well Reznor.' Culaan offered. Honestly, my friend here usually puts her opponents down in half that time.

Reznor looked from the girl to Griffin and finally returned his gaze to Culaan. He had long since sheathed his sword as had Culaan. 'Well I will call that a win for you. When do you want to find your girl?'

'I really have no idea where to start but we should start at first light. Is there a larger town or village around here?'

'There is. The Romans occupy it though. Are you wanted by the Romans?'

'Not recently.' Culaan offered and Genevieve laughed at the private jest.

****

Andronica had watched the girl fight. Her instincts were excellent. She could almost see what her opponent was thinking and it was evident in every move she made.

Andronica needed to find out more about these two strangers, but now wasn't the time. She had overheard the young man talking with Reznor about a young woman who had accompanied them but was now missing.

The stories about the pair were rife in the village. Shining weapons of power and godlike strength, but Andronica didn't believe in fairy-tales. There was more to this pair and it had something to do with the stirring of power she was feeling.

They might be waiting until morning to find the missing girl, but Andronica wasn't. She couldn't explain exactly why, but the girl was or would be leading her to the missing link. She packed her bag with provisions and touched the amulet at her neck, feeling the protective power surge through her once more.

She swung the bag over her shoulder and made her way to the barn. The young man on guard-duty stirred as she approached. She touched her hand to his temple and he slumped back onto the stool from whence he had come.

'Sleep well Tristan.' Andronica knew he would likely recall nothing but if he did, it would be that he fainted. She expected to be back before he awoke and then she would tend to him as the village Healer.

Chapter 7

Ariela knew she was dreaming. She distinctly recalled going to bed and falling asleep but this place felt so real. The moon was full and high in the sky and the trees were the same variety she had seen when she arrived.

The flat land spread out before her, as far as she could see until her eyes fell upon the moonlit mountains in the distance. The sky had an eerie glow that made the Priestess feel as though magic were floating in the air.

She turned and saw the Senator's Estate behind her and watched as the final candle-light was extinguished from the room where Constantius was convalescing. The Priestess smiled at the thought of the bruised and blackened eye that she had heard he was sporting.

'Serves you right you scoundrel.'

She realised her feet were no longer in contact with the ground and smiled at her stupidity. She had waited long enough to find her friends and using the Ethereal was the most sensible thing to do. Obviously her subconscious knew it, she had just been so busy surviving in her new surroundings she did not even think of it.

Ariela allowed her heart to lead her. She felt Culaan almost as soon as she thought of his blue eyes and broad shoulders. She allowed her spirit to be drawn to his. Her heart seemed to pound in her ears, but that was impossible. She knew her body lay vulnerable in her bed, but she shared her room with Ophelia and the servant's quarters were full of people. Besides, Constantius was sleeping off his injuries. She willed herself to remain calm.

The Priestess reached a small village on the outskirts of the region. It was a at least an hour's ride from the Senator's estate and Ariela wondered how she could possibly get away, let alone acquire a horse to make the trip to see Culaan.

Ariela felt an unusual presence that tugged at her spirit as she approached the camp. There was a large building ringed by smaller huts. In the forest that surrounded the clearing a lonely hut drew her attention. There was no one within, not anyone she could feel. The little cottage was dark as you would expect in the night, but it pulsed with an aura that concerned the Priestess. She was just about to investigate when she heard Culaan's voice.

She swung around to discover there was no one behind her. She reached out with her spirit and followed the warmth that was Culaan's soul. He was asleep in a cottage with more warriors. Culaan's voice spoke again, this time Ariela could see him.

'Where have you been beautiful? I was worried about you.'

'The Angel saw to separate us. I'm sorry but I am safe, for now.' Ariela felt Culaan's spirit stir and his body rolled in his sleep in the bunk below her. She floated above him, her smoky white essence suspended in the world between reality and the heavens.

'I'll kill anyone who harms you Ariela, you know I will.'

'I can protect myself Culaan, but I know. I've missed you.' Ariela floated down beside Culaan and reached out to touch his cheek. Her hand passed through his body, but his spirit answered. A wispy hand rose from the sleeping warrior and clasped Ariela's hand. His eyes did not open.

'What does Raziel want us to do?'

'I'm not exactly sure, but there is a woman of great power here in this time who is collecting relics, powerful objects of magic. I think we need to stop her.'

'Who is she?'

'No one knows, but when I arrived here in this village, I sensed something.'

'What?' Culaan let go of Ariela's hand and she saw his body roll again, as if his spirit was restlessly trying to wake his physical form.

'I can't say for sure, but be careful Culaan.'

'Don't go Ariela. I need to find you. Where are you?'

'I only came to make sure you and Genevieve were safe and to warn you of the woman of magic. I'll be fine Culaan. Stay and do whatever it is Raziel needs you to do.'

Ariela's spirit left to return to her body unbidden and no matter how hard she fought it, she could not stop it. A sense of panic began to rise with the hurried return.

****

Andronica arrived in the town and tried to sense the power, but it was gone. She knew it had been here. She had been drawn to it like a fox to a rabbit, but now her senses struggled to pick up any scent.

The Druid smiled as the feeling of power returned and she could see with her magic the streak of spirit that moved almost invisibly through the ethereal.

'You are powerful indeed but where have you been?'

Andronica reached out with her talent to seek the relic that she now knew remained guarded in the Senator's office. She had seen it once, when it was first unearthed. The image of it had come to her in a dream, but it had disappeared almost instantly until yesterday, when she had felt it once more.

Someone with magic had been guarding the relic or she would have been able to feel it constantly, but this newcomer was not responsible for that. The Guardians must have someone here. That meant they likely knew she was seeking Brísingamen and obtaining it would be harder than before.

Andronica touched her amulet once more. It was her protection and should shield her from discovery, but it would be unwise to steal the relic now, without fully understanding who the new wielder of magic was. She had no understanding if the newcomer willingly aided the Guardians or acted alone.

The Healer lifted her heavy linen skirt and carefully made her way into the Senator's Estate. She needed to get closer to reach out with her talent and search for both the Guardian and the powerful newcomer.

She walked through the gates, past the sentry on duty who sniffed the air as a hound dog would and searched his surroundings as though he were seeking out prey. He touched his sword-hilt reflexively and frowned in confusion as the air moved around him, but no one was visible.

Andronica smiled at his furrowed brow and kept her hand on the amulet to maintain the spell as she moved on toward the manor. The building was three storeys tall, with ancient marble stone pillars marking the entrance and intricately carved mantels framed the heavy wooden door and shuttered windows.

The grounds were carefully manicured and shone like sheets of green silk in the moonlight.

Andronica had seen the astral form return and it had not entered the main house, instead, it had flown over the building and beyond. The Healer skirted the main portico and took the winding path that led past the rear of the building and toward a barn-like structure.

She tried to peer through the windows, but the shutters were thick and the slats too closely fitted to see through. There was no light within so Andronica touched the wooden window frame and steadied herself, still with one hand on her amulet for protection.

She allowed her spirit to soar above the building and with her astral form, she could see inside the walls. There were four rooms, evenly divided by a central passageway. In the far room was a single bed with a plump woman lying flat on her back, the soft sound of snoring floating on the night air.

In the room across the hall from her were two young men, likely grounds staff or stable boys. Further down the hall from the two boys Andronica found the room she sought. Inside two young women slept.

As the Healer reached out with her spirit to delve into the mind of the first girl, the girl's eyes flew open. She peered straight at Andronica causing her to leap back and retreat to her body. She clasped the amulet tightly in the palm of her hand and grabbed a large handful of her skirt. She moved quickly toward the exit, rushing past the guard so fast his hair whipped his face with the air movement.

Andronica didn't release the amulet until she was well clear of the estate and about to mount her horse. She couldn't be sure, but she could feel eyes on her and for the first time in a very long time, Andronica felt the essence of a one-time friend left many years behind her.

Chapter 8

Dawn found Ariela and Ophelia wide awake. Their visitor had stirred both girls from their sleep.

'I don't understand why she ran so quickly?' Ariela brushed her hair and tied it back in a long braid.

'You must have scared her.' Ophelia pulled her tunic over her head as she spoke, muffling the sound of her words. 'You are very powerful you know. When I felt you throw Constantius across the room, you had me scared.' The girl's smiling face peeked from the opening in her dress.

'No, that wasn't it. For the tiniest sliver of a second I felt Morrigan with me.'

'Who is Morrigan?'

'A friend, a Druid who I was helping before I arrived here.' Ariela still struggled with the idea of flitting about through time. 'I don't understand how she *could* be with me, when she is back there.' Ariela pointed to nowhere in particular behind her and Ophelia nodded her understanding.

'You were probably just dreaming about Morrigan before the spirit arrived. How did you sense our visitor anyway, from your sleep?'

'I'd been visiting my friends—well my spirit had been. I'd just returned, more like I'd been summoned back. Maybe Morrigan summoned me?'

'Could she do that from where-ever she is?'

'I have no idea.'

'I'm not even going to ask you how you travel with your spirit. That seems outside my scope. You mentioned your friends.'

'Yes, I totally forgot to tell you. I found them and they are safe.'

Ophelia reached out and patted Ariela on the hand. 'That is good news.'

'Well yes and no. Culaan was fairly upset that I wouldn't tell him where I was.'

'Why didn't you?'

'If the Angel wanted him here with me, he would be here. There must be something he needs to do there.'

'Sounds like he'll find you anyway, with or without your help.' Ophelia smiled knowingly and Ariela scrunched her face in response. Her new friend was right. He wouldn't give up looking for her.

'Darn, I should have told him. You're right, he will stumble right into the middle of something trying to find me.'

'Alexandria, Ophelia. Where in the blazes are you two?' Katerina hollered from the hallway before pounding on the door.

'Remember not to annoy her. She's stronger than she looks.'

'But I can throw Emperor's sons across the room!'
Ariela announced and both girls giggled as Ophelia
opened the door with a curtsy.

'Sorry Mistress, we are on our way now.'

'You best rush child. Constantius is up and about
and in fine form.' Katerina looked at Ariela over
Ophelia's shoulder. 'And you miss, you had best make
yourself invisible. He keeps ranting something about you
throwing him across the room or some rubbish like that.
You won't reason with him either, the boy is out of his
mind.'

'Yes Mistress. Where do you want me working
today then?'

'Stay in the cookhouse. At least if he finds you
there, you won't be on your own.'

'Yes Mistress.' Ariela curtsied and both girls
rushed down the hallway.

'Don't you hate all that curtsying and grovelling...
being royal and all.'

'No, it's quite good really. When I was in Shiloh, I
was a Priestess, but still a Princess. I was never treated
like everyone else. At least here, I'm just another slave.'
Ariela smiled and Ophelia burst out laughing.

'Spoken like a powerful magic wielding slave —
someone who can throw budding Emperors across the
room with a flick of her wrist.'

Ariela shrugged with a smile. 'Well there is that of
course.'

****

Culaan couldn't sleep after Ariela's visit. The sun was yet to crest the mountains and dawn was still some time away judging by the lack of bird sounds.

The warrior had dressed early and headed out to get some fresh air. Sleeping in the bunk house with a dozen men wasn't something he was accustomed to and the smell was growing irritating.

'Damn you woman, why didn't you tell me where you are?'

'I am just behind you.' Genevieve smiled as Culaan swung round with a shocked expression. 'You *are* away with the fairies, aren't you? You didn't even hear me approaching.'

'I was thinking of Ariela.' Genevieve forced a smile. She sighed and slapped Culaan on the shoulder.

'Want to do some sparring?'

Culaan shook his head, his face long and sad. Genevieve sighed again and scrunched her lips as she thought. 'You know you are such a lost puppy. Seriously, where did Culaan the great warrior go? Culaan, the toss-women-aside-like-dog-bones tough guy disappear to?'

Culaan broke into a grin at his friend's attempt to cheer him up. 'You are the only person I know who can insult someone and make it sound like a compliment.' Culaan heard something and looked to Genevieve for confirmation. The Huntress nodded and they both slowly made their way through the undergrowth toward the noise.

The stable boy was unconscious on the stool outside the doorway and Culaan put his hand on the hilt of his sword reflexively while Genevieve carefully lifted her bow from her shoulder.

He raised an eyebrow in the soft moonlight and she shrugged her answer. He should know she rarely left the cabin without it.

The sound of stomping horse hooves and a soft neighing drew the warrior's attention back to the barn. *Was someone trying to steal horses?*

Before Culaan had time to react, he saw the source of the disturbance. The Healer moved through the doorway touching the slumped guard on the cheek gently as she passed. The boy sprang to his feet like a jack-rabbit and looked around as though he had forgotten where he was.

'Tristan. Are you feeling alright?' Andronica asked with false innocence.

'I, I don't know. What happened?' The boy looked more confused than before.

'I think you might have nodded off. Don't worry. I won't tell anyone. Your secret is safe with me.' Andronica walked away without further comment, not trying to hide her smile. Her back was to Tristan, he would have no idea, but both Culaan and Genevieve saw.

The warriors waited until Andronica was out of sight before speaking. 'What was that all about?' Genevieve frowned as the question left her lips.

'It might have something to do with what Ariela was talking about.'

'What was she talking about?'

'There isn't much to explain yet, except magic is involved. It might be worth talking with the boy.'

'Not likely. He was out to it when we arrived and even if he did know something, he won't tell us. Reznor will skin him alive if he finds out the boy was asleep at his post.'

'True, but we need to keep an eye on Andronica. Ariela said she felt magic here and you saw what the Healer just did to the boy. You follow after her and see what she does next while I take a look at her horse and see if I can figure out where she went.'

'Good thinking. Have a casual chat with the stable boy and see if he lets anything slip. It will keep your mind off Ariela.' Genevieve smiled.

'Oh, thanks for that. You had to go there didn't you. Now I'm worried sick about her again.'

'Seriously. She wields the power of the gods and you're worried about her. We get shining weapons; she throws fireballs for goodness' sake.' Genevieve laughed quietly as she followed their suspicious Healer.

Chapter 9

Ariela stared at her wrinkled hands and smiled. 'I've never peeled this many potatoes in my whole life!'

'Now why doesn't that surprise me?'

Ariela jumped at the voice she recognised as Constantius before slowly turning to face him. She peered over his shoulder to catch sight of the cook but found him nowhere.

'You won't find anyone here. I took care of the staff. I'd like to pick up where we left off last time.'

'Which part, before or after you passed out?' Ariela wasn't afraid of Constantius. She was more concerned that she might cause him serious injury if he kept pushing her.

'I've told people what you did you know.'

'And how did that go for you? You'll be lucky if they don't find somewhere even more remote to hide you away. You know they think you're just a little insane.' Ariela twirled her finger by her temple and rolled her eyes wildly.

Constantius slumped his shoulders and sighed.

'You can't always have exactly what you want you know! I have a boyfriend and to be honest, he'd likely tear you to pieces Emperor's son or not if I tell him what you've done. Why keep pushing it?'

Constantius looked at Ariela as though he were contemplating something. 'You have no idea what it feels like to be the son of the Emperor of Rome!'

'It feels like you can't be yourself. Like everyone is judging you. That every move you make is being scrutinised, gossiped about or assessed by your peers.' Ariela turned away from Constantius and collected another potato from the wooden bar and began peeling it.

Constantius stared open-mouthed at her back until he finally got a hold of himself. 'How? How could you know?'

'It's a long story and one I'm not prepared to share right now but I get it. Right now it doesn't matter. Being royal doesn't give you the right to take whatever you want.'

Constantius joined Ariela at the bench, picked up a potato and studied it as though seeing it for the first time.

'Do you want to help?' Ariela smiled as she passed a peeling knife to the young man. Constantius watched as Ariela peeled the potato and began mirroring her movements.

'I can't control my moods. I don't understand why!'

Ariela waited trying to find the right words. The last thing she wanted to do was upset him again.

'It wasn't too bad really but the Senator suggested I call in a local healer. I wouldn't usually enlist help from the local Goth tribes but this woman wasn't one of them.'

'What happened?' Ariela encouraged Constantius carefully, her mind running over what he was saying and wondering what it had to do with the woman who'd visited and the Goth village Culaan had found himself in.

'It got worse. So much worse.'

'Did you stop seeing the Healer?'

'I did, for a while, and it started to get better but now it's worse again.'

'What did the Healer use to treat you?' Ariela was curious. She knew she might be pushing her luck but she needed to know.

'I don't know. It was a crushed herb. She told me to put it in hot water and drink it in the mornings. She said it would keep me calmer.'

'What did it look like?' Ariela took the now peeled potato from Constantius and began chopping up the large pile she had in front of her.

'What are you doing here Sir?' Katerina's tone was careful as she looked from Ariela to Constantius. She frowned in confusion at the relaxed atmosphere that greeted her.

'Alexandria was showing me how to peel potatoes. Very educational, but I was just leaving.' Constantius bowed to Ariela and then slipped past the narrow wooden bench and squeezed around Katerina to make his way from the cookhouse and into the main dining room.

'What was that all about? Yesterday he was raving on about you being the Devil incarnate! You watch him Alexandria. Mark my words, he will be trouble.'

Ariela smiled at the motherly advice. 'I'm just trying to keep him calm Mistress. No one wants to get the crazy boy all riled up, least of all me.'

Ophelia came into the cookhouse and heard the last few words of Ariela's conversation and cringed. Constantius had been waiting just outside the door and would have heard every word.

Katerina walked past her out of the cookhouse and Ophelia's face fell.

'What?' Ariela asked genuinely worried.

'He heard you.'

'Who?'

'Constantius. I heard you and he was just outside the door. He must have heard you call him crazy. What was he doing here again anyway?'

'Oh no! I was finally getting somewhere and now he will be out for blood again.'

Chapter 10

The young man made his way to his rooms. He was greeted with darkness and suddenly felt the reflection in his soul. There was a rich red coloured chair in the corner, dark wooden furniture, a large heavy four poster bed covered with a chocolate-brown bedspread and even the rugs were oppressively dark.

He stomped over to the tall window covered in almost black curtains and tore them from the rod. Constantius could feel the rage returning and he wanted more than anything to stay calm. He could hardly blame the girl for calling him crazy. He was after all quite unreliable with his moods.

The light streamed into the room, casting eerie shadows that further assaulted the would-be Emperor's mood. He pulled the drawer of his side dresser out with haste and searched for the powder the Healer had given him. He found it and without bothering to boil water or measure out the dose, he took a handful and threw it into his mouth.

He chewed it slowly, trying to make it go down his tight throat as his saliva finally made it pasty enough to swallow.

His vision filled with swaying red creatures as his chair seemed to come to life and walk across the room at him. Panic rippled through his mind as he scrambled to get away from the red Devil that was trying to kill him.

****

Culaan sat down next to Genevieve who was deep in conversation with Griffin. The young Goth warrior made eye contact with Culaan and smiled until he read the message in his ice-blue eyes.

He looked at Genevieve and rose to leave the table, his hand lingering on hers while his eyes spoke of his regret. The Huntress followed his retreating back with obvious displeasure. 'That isn't fair you know. You have Ariela, can't you let me have some fun too?'

Culaan looked from his friend to the departing Griffin and sighed. 'I'm sorry. I was so focussed on finding out what you had discovered, I didn't think.'

'No, you didn't think. That seems to be a repetitive pattern with you lately.'

'Come on Genie. Calm down. I'm sure if he is worth your effort he'll be back.'

Genevieve seemed to relax. 'No, you're right. If he fears you, he's no use to me anyway. You're not going anywhere any time soon. Where you go, I go.'

'Where did the Healer go after she left the stables?'

'Just back to her little hut on the edge of the forest. She gives me the creeps that woman. Don't ask me why. What did you find out at the stable?'

'The boy's name is Tristan. He didn't have much to say really, just rubbed his head when I asked him why the horse had mud on its hooves. He said he must have forgotten to clean her up after her last ride.'

'Any idea where the Healer took the horse?'

'Well Tristan said he had gone on duty around the twelfth hour and we were out by the stables I would say around two hours before sunrise, so wherever the Healer went it was less than two hours each way.'

'Nice to know your adding has improved since we were children.' Genevieve punched her friend on the arm and laughed at her own jest.

'Reznor said there is a town about that distance from here, so let's see where she went. We can look for Ariela at the same time and apparently, the Romans occupy the territory so we might even get a little fun in the bargain.'

'I was already planning a little fun before. Remember? You interrupted me.'

'Stop pouting. This will be much better. We can find some Roman centurions to pick a fight with.'

Chapter 11

'What should I do?' Ariela paced the cookhouse.

'You'll wear a hole in the floor if you keep that up.' Ophelia smiled. 'He'll get over it. He really isn't your problem. We have more important things to worry about. We need to discover who visited last night and where to find her.'

'I don't understand how you haven't discovered who she is yet. You know so much about her, what she wants but not who she is.'

'We can track her, or her magic, but she has been very careful not to reveal herself. Last night was the first time she has slipped up.'

'I still need to check on Constantius. I'm worried about him. He said a Healer has been giving him powder to keep him calm, but I have a strange feeling he's being drugged.'

'Why would anyone drug that dimwit?'

'He is the next Emperor and he is currently chasing Brísingamen with great zeal. I think that is too much of a coincidence, don't you?' Ariela lifted her eyebrow to emphasise her concern.

Ophelia scrunched her nose and twisted her lip as she thought. 'You might be right. We should find out who the Healer is. I'll check in on him.'

'Better you than me I think.'

****

Ariela left the cookhouse, her duties finally done for the day. The shadows were growing long and the cool of the evening was beginning to settle in.

The Priestess made her way down the winding path to the common bunkhouse she shared with the other slaves. She quickly changed into a training tunic and slipped back out of the room, trying to remain anonymous.

As she made her way past the dormitory to the forest beyond, she couldn't help but feel someone was watching her. Ariela took a look over her shoulder as she rounded the building, but saw nothing. It didn't provide her with any assurance and she wondered if she should have collected up a dagger before heading into the darkening forest.

****

Constantius tried to push the confusion from his mind. His vision swam and his thoughts felt even more jumbled than usual. He walked to the window and opened the shutters in search of fresh air.

He watched Ariela, her slim body firing his imagination in the light tunic she wore. Her tanned skin glistening in the light of the setting sun sent shivers down the young noble's back.

A glaze formed in his eyes that forced the real images to the back as his vison swam with thoughts of

Ariela. 'I will have you woman. You will writhe beneath me and your screams will ignite my soul.' Constantius closed the shutters and collected his weapon, sliding it into the sword-sheath with a stiff, ungainly motion.

He opened the door hastily, his vision focussed on another place, he almost sent Ophelia sliding across the hallway with his body weight as he barged through the doorway.

'My Lord, forgive me.' Ophelia curtsied, head bowed submissively. As she rose to see if her apology had been accepted, she was met with a steely gaze and almost black eyes. Constantius's pupils were so dilated there was no iris left.

He carried on, his course undeterred, his vision focussed beyond Ophelia as though she never existed. The servant frowned as she stepped aside, allowing him unrestricted passage.

Her skin crawled with unrestrained fear and as Constantius strode down the stairs and out the front door, a cold sensation ran down the young woman's back.

'Ariela!' She gasped and set off in pursuit, carefully maintaining a safe distance.

****

Ariela stretched her neck from side to side before she began her warm up. She gently swung her arms across her body and then in circles backwards, then forwards. She lunged to the side, relaxing her inner thighs on both sides before reaching down to touch her toes. She clasped her ankles and pulled her face to her knees, holding the position as long as she could stand to.

The routine continued with jumps, a few tumbles and sideways stretches before she felt the warmth of her body and the trickle of beads of sweat down her chest.

The Priestess found a long thin branch and began to swing it in wide arcs across her body before twirling it at a speed too difficult to see.

'I miss you so much Salaman. I could really do with a real training session right now. I'm so out of practice.'

'I'm sure I can help you with that.' Constantius strode into the small clearing Ariela trained in. The area was surrounded by trees and brush, the remains of a small camp fire being the only thing that occupied the tiny space around her.

'Constantius.' Ariela watched the young man closely. His features were hard to make out in the dying sunlight, but Ariela didn't need to see his face. His tone spoke volumes.

'I'm sorry if I upset you. I was only saying that to get the Mistress to leave me be. You understand, don't you?'

'I don't care what you think of me. I'll take you with or without your permission.'

'Take me?' Ariela knew what he meant but she wanted to try and engage him in conversation — to reason with him — to give him time to calm down.

'Yes. I'm going to enjoy the feel of you beneath me.' Constantius drew his sword and swung it around his wrist as Ariela watched it carefully.

'I don't want to hurt you Constantius. You know I can.' Ariela put her hands up, palms out in front of her,

her makeshift cane still held with one thumb, limp and unthreatening.

'Your power won't work on me this time witch.'

'Please Constantius.' Ariela had no time to continue her pleading before her staff reflexively sprang to protect her from the attack. 'I won't use my power this time. I don't want to risk hurting you. You know I never meant to hurt you.'

Constantius didn't answer, instead he smirked in a way that failed to soften his features and advanced on the Priestess.

Chapter 12

'You haven't lost the trail, have you?' Culaan rubbed his chin as he watched Genevieve flick a twig from what looked like a horse's hoof print.

'Of course not.' Genevieve didn't attempt to hide her agitation.

'I was only asking.' Culaan lifted his hands in front of him defensively.

'It leads into that Estate.' Genevieve pointed to the three-storey building with a stone wall and metal spiked fence surrounding it.

'So, what is the Healer doing visiting such a fancy place?'

'I don't know. Why don't you go up and ask that nice guard over there?' Genevieve teased.

'You're in fine form tonight, aren't you?'

'Well you did interrupt my entertainment to drag me out into the chill of the evening to track in near darkness. Excuse me for being a little testy.'

'Come on. You're just as curious about what that weird woman is up to as I am and aren't you even slightly worried about Ariela?'

Genevieve sighed. 'Of course I am.'

'Did you hear that?'

'No?'

'Follow me. I heard something.' Culaan began to run around the perimeter of the Estate, just inside the treeline where the guards wouldn't notice them. The sound of grunts and weapons clashing came to them as they reached the far side of the grounds.

'You must have heard that!' Culaan challenged.

'No! I've grown deaf in my old age.' Genevieve pushed past her friend and carefully studied the tracks that lead from the rear gate of the estate to the forest beyond.

'What is it?' Culaan fingered his weapon but hadn't drawn it yet. It would light the growing darkness and alert everyone to their presence so he fought the temptation. He was still learning to bring the silver light on demand.

'Footprints, without horses, just two, probably three people.' Genevieve followed the trail into the forest, Culaan following closely behind as the Huntress pushed the undergrowth open slightly to get a better view. She gasped and Culaan pushed past her to get a closer look. His sword was in his hand before he knew what had happened and both he and Genevieve were standing inside the clearing.

A young woman was on the ground, bleeding from a cut to her temple. Beyond her another woman swung a staff at her assailant, striking home between wild sword swings from her enemy.

'Ariela!' Culaan had recognised her immediately. A smile crept across his face as her attacker's eyes grew wide at the sight of his glowing sword. 'Step away from my woman or face the consequences.' He strode toward Ariela with a crazed expression, lit by his fiery sword. The effect was frightening.

'Don't hurt him Culaan.' Ariela called over her shoulder without taking her eyes off Constantius.

'Don't hurt him? Are you mad? He's trying to kill you!'

Genevieve had returned her bow to her shoulder before it even lifted clear and smiled at the exchange.

'You know she throws fire balls Culaan. If she wanted him dead, he'd be dead already.'

Reason seemed to reach her broad-shouldered friend and he lowered his sword arm, the glowing weapon still unsheathed.

'Constantius, you are surrounded now. Please put that sword away, before I have to really hurt you.' Ariela pleaded

'If she doesn't I certainly will.' Culaan warned.

Constantius looked from the shining sword to Ariela and suddenly seemed to focus on Ophelia, unconscious on the ground. His face broke out in a sweat, barely visible with the light shining from Culaan's weapon.

He slumped to the ground in apparent surrender but it didn't take Ariela long to realise he had fainted.

'Culaan, help me.' Ariela ran to her attacker and Culaan leapt to stop her. He was too late and before he knew it, the Priestess was lifting Constantius's head and resting it in her lap.

Culaan looked from Ariela to Genevieve who
returned his gaze with a raised eyebrow. The warrior
hadn't sheathed his sword, instead he held it aloft to aid
in the growing darkness.

'What in the goddess's name are you doing? He
just tried to kill you and who is he anyway?' The
jealously was plain in his words, but Ariela chose to
ignore it.

Genevieve finally uncrossed her arms and shook
her head. 'Only you could forgive someone who just
tried to run you through with his sword.' She laughed.
'I'll check the girl.' She went to Ophelia who was
beginning to regain consciousness.

'He is sick. Someone has been poisoning him.'

Chapter 13

'We can't take him back to the Estate like this. The Senator will have questions and Katerina is reasonable, but I doubt she will think bringing an unconscious noble back in the darkness as reasonable.'

'Ariela, you are going to have to explain a few things first. Do you mean that Estate?' Culaan pointed behind them.

'Culaan, we don't have time for me to explain anything just yet. Where can we take Constantius before day break, where he can be safe and Ophelia and I can get back to the Estate unnoticed?'

Culaan frowned and finally sheathed his sword. 'We could take him back to the village.'

'Will they shelter a Roman?' Genevieve asked across the clearing as she helped Ophelia to her feet.

'Why not? I am Thor, their god after all.' Culaan's smile was invisible in the darkness.

'Now who needs to do some explaining?' Ariela challenged.

'We'll take him, but he won't be happy when he wakes up far from home. We'll have to restrain him.'

Genevieve offered as she came closer to inspect their patient in what little moonlight had risen.

'No, you can't restrain him. He is sick. Someone has been feeding him herbs from a village nearby. Herbs that make his mind weak. I think the same woman visited me last night.'

'Now *that* complicates things.' Culaan bent down low and lifted Constantius over his broad shoulder.

'We tracked a woman from the village, a wise woman. She left late last night and we thought something wasn't quite right.'

'In that case, we can't take Constantius to the village either. If your wise woman is the same Healer who has been drugging the son of the Emperor of Rome, then he won't be safe there either.' Ariela touched Constantius's forehead. Culaan forced down his jealousy once more.

He turned to face the Priestess, and with each movement the warrior made the Roman noble's head flopped on his back like a dead deer. He stepped closer to Ariela and she responded with a touch of her open palm on his cheek.

'I've missed you,' he whispered. 'Should I be worried about this sack?' He indicated Constantius on his back.

'Never!' The Priestess lifted to her toes and kissed him gently on the lips.

'Hmmm! Really! Time and a place people.' Genevieve interrupted.

'Oh, I don't know. There's always time for a little love.' Ophelia had regained her composure and smiled at the couple.

Genevieve turned to the stranger and grimaced. 'You just suffered a knock to the head. Your judgement can hardly be clear.'

'My judgement is just fine. I'd have taken the opportunity, wouldn't you?' Ophelia winked as she whispered so only Genevieve could hear, her eyes remaining on the tall, broad-shouldered warrior.

The Huntress drew a deep breath and smiled. Ophelia saw the wistful look and patted her on the shoulder gently. 'We need to get that sack you speak of, somewhere safe before he wakes up. Any ideas?'

'We are all new here Ophelia, you lead the way.' Ariela suggested, her attention finally drawn from Culaan's unshaven cheeks and warm lips.

'Do you think we can sneak him into our servant quarters?'

Ariela shook her head. 'No, Katerina might find him there and we need to keep someone with him until he regains consciousness.'

'I'll find a cave nearby. We'll hold him there and I'll come back and show you where we are. You can then come and try to make some sense of why the Healer would be drugging the son of the Emperor.'

'We have a fairly good idea, but we need to get back to the Estate before anyone notices we are missing.'

'Ariela, we will have to restrain him if he wakes up. Without anyone he knows there, he isn't going to be in any condition to reason with.'

Ariela nodded her understanding. 'Just don't hurt him Culaan. That woman has been messing with his sanity for a while.'

Chapter 14

'So! Do you think something has been going on between them?' Culaan set Constantius down without too much care, his head flopped and hit the ground firmly.

'Be careful. We don't want to kill him with a head injury.' Genevieve knelt to readjust the man's fine clothing and use his cape to make a pillow for his head.

'What is it with you women? Fussing over him like he is a baby. A little smack to the head will keep him quiet longer is all.' Culaan scowled.

'Oh stop it will you! There is nothing going on. Ariela is just kind and caring and she could have killed the little pain in the butt but she obviously doesn't see the need. Or more importantly, she doesn't want to raise any alarm at the Estate. She's obviously discovered something.'

'Yes, and she isn't telling us!'

'You are such a little pup at times Culaan. She will when she can. You just don't like not being in charge.'

'I'll go get some firewood or something. Keep him quiet if he wakes up.' Culaan ducked through the entrance to the cave and headed out to get some fresh air.

The sight of anyone who drew Ariela's feelings away from him, even if it was plutonic, was driving him to distraction.

They had barely had a moment to themselves. The battles before they had left his homeland had occupied all their time. Now they had been separated since arriving in this new time and he wanted Ariela—her lips—her body—her undivided attention, more than he wanted to breathe.

His entire soul was on fire, not to mention his groin and now she was back in the Senator's Estate fulfilling whatever the Angel wanted her to do, while he was stuck baby-sitting a complete stranger—one Ariela obviously cared about.

****

'So that's your boyfriend! Wow!' Ophelia teased once they finally made their way back to their rooms in the darkness. The soft snoring from Katerina could be heard as they tip-toed around trying to not disturb her.

'That's him, and I miss him so much.' Ariela sighed as she slumped onto her firm bed.

'Why didn't you stay with him? Why come back to help me and not just run away and forget all this?' Ophelia sat down on her bed and untied her tightly-laced sandals, throwing them across the room without care. They thudded against the wall and both girls giggled, waiting to see if they had awoken anyone in the night.

'Because I'm obviously here to make sure that woman doesn't kill Constantius or steel Brísingamen. You said so yourself, it's dangerous in the wrong hands.'

'It is but I'm beginning to wonder how we are going to get a hold of it before she does. She was obviously here to find a way when you felt her watching you.'

'When Constantius wakes, and he has his senses back, I'll try to reason with him.'

The laughter rang out louder than Ophelia intended and she clamped her mouth shut, her eyes wide with horror. Ariela smiled in understanding. 'Don't be so pessimistic. The Angel is with us,' she whispered. Ophelia nodded as she took her hand away from her lips. 'But I'm curious who this Healer is and why or how she is travelling through time.'

'She must have another relic she uses.' Ophelia offered.

'Yes, exactly and once we have the Brísingamen, I'll be getting Culaan to help me find out exactly what that is.'

****

Culaan walked back toward the cave, cradling an armful of carefully selected wood from small twigs to larger logs. The sound coming from the entrance made him drop the bundle and run at full speed, sword-drawn without thought of the light it would produce.

As he drew closer to the entrance, he failed at first to understand why the cave held a soft glow of light until he thought of Genevieve's bow. He took the last few steps more cautiously, expecting an altercation but it only took him a moment longer to realise the sounds drifting to his ears were no cause for alarm.

He sheathed his sword, smiling at the sounds of heavy breathing and soft moans that left nothing to the imagination. 'Now that is one way to keep him subdued Genie.'

Instead of staying to eavesdrop on his friend, he decided he would get back to the Estate so he could keep Ariela informed. She would have to be up soon, as the pre-dawn chill had set in and servants were always early to rise to serve their masters.

Culaan was growing agitated. There was little or no chance he was going to be able to sneak past the guard in broad daylight. He sat near the clearing he had left Ariela in the night before and waited, hoping she would find a way to get to him.

The afternoon sun created long shadows on the forest floor and Culaan considered if waiting was the right choice. Genevieve was now alone with the noble born crazy man and although she seemed to have him under control when he left, he realised anything could have happened since then.

'Are you brooding still?' Culaan jumped before Ariela's voice registered. She giggled. 'Culaan, it's not like you to be so distracted. I could have been a guard.'

'You're right. You drive me to distraction woman.' Ariela moved into his open arms and relaxed into his strong embrace. 'What I wouldn't do to take my time with you right now.'

Ariela smiled as she kissed him gently on the lips. The warmth lingered between them, their lips touching softly for a moment longer. 'I wish we could. But you need to tell me where Constantius is. I'll bring Ophelia tonight, after everyone is in bed.'

'We found a cave about an hour's walk north of here. Follow the main track until you come to a large boulder. Head up into the forest to your left. You'll see an outcrop of more rocks ahead. I'll keep an eye out for you.'

'We'll be there. Is Constantius alright?'

Culaan smiled mischievously. 'Genevieve has him under control.' Ariela frowned and Culaan chuckled softly. 'She definitely hasn't hurt him. You don't need to worry. She is taking very good care of him.'

'I'm not sure I like the sound of that.' Ariela stretched on her toes again and kissed Culaan on the cheek. 'I'll see you a few hours after dark.'

'You'd better. If I don't see you coming my way, I'll be back here to get you.'

'We'll be there.'

Chapter 15

Culaan entered the cave casually and smiled as he saw Genevieve sitting by a small fire made from the firewood he had abandoned outside the cave.

'Thanks for collecting this.' Genevieve pointed to the fire. 'Did you bring back any food?'

Culaan lifted a small hare. 'It isn't much, but Ariela will bring more tonight.' He tossed the animal to the Huntress. 'You're the expert. I left the skinning to you. I know how much you hate it when I put holes in the hide or leave fur on the meat.'

'You've got that right.'

'How's he doing?' Culaan nodded to the sleeping prisoner.

'He is fine.'

'I bet he is!' Culaan grinned at Genevieve's innocent demeanour. 'Did you have fun?'

'I told you that you interrupted my early plans. He was in the right place at the right time and he is relaxed isn't he?'

'I'm not complaining. Did he tell you anything?'

'We weren't exactly talking about much. But he seems to be free of the drug now.'

'I'll wake him up and see if we can get more answers then.' Culaan walked over to Constantius while Genevieve carefully skinned the hare and threaded it onto a thin stick left amongst the firewood Culaan had collected earlier. He kicked the prisoner gently on the leg, keeping his distance in case the man wasn't as docile as he seemed.

'Huh!' Constantius jumped awake.

'You sleep well for a madman.'

'Madman? Who are you?' Constantius rubbed his head in confusion, trying to take in his surroundings once more.

'How much of last night do you remember?'

'I remember her.' Constantius nodded to Genevieve.

'What about attacking Ariela?'

'Who is Ariela?'

'The girl from the Estate. The one you attacked in the forest. Don't you remember?' Culaan fought the urge to lift the man to his feet.

'I don't think he remembers much. Let's wait until the girls get here later.' Genevieve touched Culaan on the arm and drew him away. 'I don't think he knows Ariela by her real name. Let's wait and see what she has told him.' Genevieve whispered as they moved back to the fire.

'Who are you and why am I here?'

'Well Genevieve and you have already become acquainted.' Genie punched Culaan in the arm as he smirked. 'My name is Culaan but the locals call me Thor.'

'The god?'

'One and the same.'

'So am I a hostage? Do you plan on asking a ransom from my father?'

'No and no.' Culaan reached down and collected a skin-full of water from the small stores they had brought with them. He drank deeply and lowered himself to his haunches, taking a deep breath and smelling the aroma of the now slowly cooking hare.

'So I can leave?' Constantius queried, shifting nervously in his position against the wall of the cave.

'You can leave but my friend wants to talk to you about a few things. Did you know you went berserk last night? You nearly killed an unarmed girl with your sword. You threw one against the ground and nearly killed her too.'

Culaan studied the young noble's face carefully. He looked genuinely appalled by what he was listening to. 'I couldn't have.'

'You did. I saw it with my own eyes. Apparently, you were under the influence of a drug, something the Healer of the local Goth village had given you. My friend thinks she knows why and since you don't recall anything, it might be a good idea for you to hang around and discover what she knows. What do you say?'

Constantius looked from Genevieve to Culaan and back to Genevieve. She smiled softly at the confused look on his face. She left turning the hare on the fire, the smoke drifting softly out the cave entrance, and walked over to sit beside Constantius. She nodded in the direction of the fire and Culaan took over turning the meat.

'We don't mean you any harm. In fact, I kind of enjoy your company. Don't you enjoy mine?'

Constantius smiled involuntarily, the memory of Genevieve's warm lips on his, fresh in his mind. 'I can't recall. Maybe you can remind me?'

Genevieve lent in and kissed the nobleman firmly on the lips.

Chapter 16

'Where is the one you call Thor?' Andronica challenged as she tapped Reznor on the chest with one finger. The big warrior caught her hand and held it out in front of him firmly.

'I don't answer to you Healer. You answer to me.'

'You have no idea who you are dealing with. The newcomer and his girlfriend. Where are they?'

'How should I know? I'm not their keeper. They were here last night. Maybe they took horses somewhere. Ask Tristan, he might know.' Reznor frowned at the woman. She seemed to have gone quite mad.

'You need to send men out to track them. They are dangerous.'

'I won't do that Andronica. They are gods, more powerful than any warrior we have in our midst. They can do whatever they want to as far as I'm concerned. When the time comes for me to need their help, the last thing I want is to have angered them.'

Andronica took a deep breath as though she were about to explode. The vein on her forehead pulsed and she wiggled her fingers like they were digging into unseen enemies. Reznor backed away slightly but the

Healer didn't pursue him. Instead she spun on her heel and stormed from the clearing toward her isolated hut.

Reznor stared at her back and waved Griffin over. 'Keep your eyes on that woman Griff. Something is off.'

'I'm not ashamed to say she scares me a little.' Griffin grinned and Reznor chuckled.

'You're only human man. She's a worry for sure. Report back what she gets up to and our Thor and Skathi too if you happen to stumble across them. My instincts have been telling me that something very strange is going on with our Healer and it's only been getting worse since our friends arrived.'

****

Andronica asked Tristan what he knew and that was very little. The warrior now known as Thor had asked him questions about the horse she had used when she visited the town, but other than that, he knew nothing. She was sure of it. Even probing his mind drew a blank.

The Druid fingered her protective amulet and returned to her cottage. She pulled her mattress off the bed and opened the hidden door. She rummaged deep into the depths of the dark storage compartment and finally found what she was looking for.

The ring was made of bone and etched with symbols. She slid it carefully onto her index finger and made a fist. She gripped her amulet once more and replaced the lid on her hiding place, pulling the mattress back on top carefully. She stepped back and examined the bed, then moved forward and adjusted the quilt before turning and leaving the cottage.

The Druid made her way to the stables, this time the need for stealth unnecessary. It was daylight and she was past worrying about what the villagers knew.

****

Ariela returned to the Estate in time to see a woman riding through the main gates as though she belonged there. The hair on the back of her neck tingled and the feeling of the woman's essence was unmistakable. The Priestess ducked out of sight quickly and made her way into the cookhouse.

'About time you got back.' Ophelia challenged, her hands placed firmly on her hips.

'The Healer is here. I just saw her ride up. Has she been here before?'

'Once or twice. That's how she discovered the Brísingamen I guess.'

'Well Constantius isn't here, so who is she here to see?'

'Maybe she doesn't know he isn't here. This could be interesting. We should go take a look.'

'She would recognise me and she knows I will recognise her. No, you should go. See if you can clean the hallway outside the Senator's office. She must plan on going there.'

'Will do. Don't get too far away though. I might need help.'

'No, whatever you do, don't engage her.'

'But what if she gets the Brísingamen from the Senator?'

Ariela chewed her lip a moment. 'Well, I guess you better come and get me if you think that is about to happen. I'm not sure if I'm powerful enough to stop her, but we can't let her get a hold of it.'

Ophelia nodded. 'You've got that right. Hopefully she is here for Constantius.'

'Hopefully.' Ariela busied herself tidying the work bench and making room for meal preparations. She watched Ophelia smooth her skirts, collect a cleaning rag and duck out of the main cookhouse doorway that adjoined the Senator's dining hall.

Ophelia grinned as she left the cookhouse and Ariela returned the smile with more confidence than she was feeling. How was she going to fight this Druid? What did Raziel want of her? Was it really to stop her getting Brísingamen? Maybe she was missing something.

Chapter 17

'Excuse me Sir. The Lady Andronica to see you.' Katerina bowed as the Healer strode past her, the skirt of her fine dress swaying vigorously as she walked.

The Senator rose slightly from his seat, a look of mild curiosity creased his forehead. 'To what do I owe the pleasure Andronica? Constantius isn't here today.' There was a tone about his voice that indicated he knew the two shared some type of relationship.

'I'm not here for the noble boy today Senator. I am here for you.' The Healer waited for the Senator to offer her a seat, which he finally did after obviously carefully considering his options.

He walked around his desk and pulled out a wooden chair with soft fabric that crunched slightly as Andronica took her seat. 'I'm listening,' was all he said as he returned to his own chair, pulling it into the desk protectively before crossing his fingers in a temple like fashion on the desk.

Andronica smiled. He knew she was a powerful Healer and the division of the desk was his way of making himself feel safe and secure. 'The Goth tribes are planning something. I'm not entirely sure what yet, but I wanted to offer my services to you, the true rulers of this region.'

The Senator's eyes grew wide for only a heartbeat before he composed himself. 'And what do you hope for in return?'

'Nothing of great value really.'

'So, you don't want the relic I keep in the cupboard over there?' The Senator teased, as Andronica's eyes looked over his shoulder and lingered on the closed door.

'Well if you are offering, I wouldn't dream of refusing of course.'

****

Ophelia dusted the railing of the stairwell before making her way along the hall to the door of the Senator's office. She wiped the timber door slowly and meticulously as she leant her ear against it.

She risked peering again through the key-hole for only a moment before double checking over her shoulder to ensure she wasn't seen. She could feel the magic emanating from the Healer. It wasn't strong like Ariela's, but it was constant and she took another look to see if the cupboard had been opened, but it hadn't.

As she squirmed to get a better position to see through the key-way, she saw the burgundy skirt of Andronica's dress reach the door. She quickly crossed the hall to the doorway on the other side and began dusting furiously.

The Senator's office door swung open. 'I'll be in touch when I know more Senator.' Andronica stopped speaking when she saw Ophelia in the hall. She frowned at the young servant as though assessing the danger and then curtsied to the Senator before pulling the office door closed.

Ophelia deliberately avoided any eye contact with the Healer. She kept her back to the Senator's Office and focussed on the door in front of her. She looked at the carving, trying to memorise the scene. Her skin crawled with the rise in magic released as Andronica began searching Ophelia's mind. The young Guardian couldn't risk using any protection, instead she continued to focus on the beautiful wood, the shining finish, the rough edges of the carving and the polished brass of the handle.

The woman continued to interrogate her mind with magic but finally turned and left the servant to her duties.

Ophelia could feel the sweat dripping down her back. She let out her breath slowly and tried to remind herself to breathe again. Andronica held her skirt as she descended the stairs. She brushed past Katerina without a word and reached the front steps before Ophelia finally moved from the wooden door she had been so focussed on.

She ran the cloth down the balustrade as she took the stairs two at a time. She nearly barrelled Katerina from her feet as she rushed to report back to Ariela.

'Where are you going in such a hurry?'

'Oh sorry Mistress. I need to help Ar..Alexandria.' She couldn't believe she nearly used the Priestess's real name. She was growing too familiar but she couldn't stop herself.

'Have you finished the dusting? I'm not sure you've eavesdropped quite enough yet!' Katerina challenged.

'Mistress?'

'You heard me. I saw you on your knees peering through the Senator's study door. What did you discover?'

Ophelia frowned unsure exactly what the Mistress was asking. If she admitted to eavesdropping would she be punished, or did Katerina actually want to know what was going on?

Katerina grabbed Ophelia by the arm and pulled her off into the cookhouse. Ariela took one look at the pained expression on her friend's face and stopped what she was doing.

'Now young lady. You and our new little friend here are going to tell me what is going on. Do you really think I didn't know you were out most of last evening? Do you,' Katerina pointed a finger at Ariela while she still held Ophelia firmly by her arm, '*really* think I didn't notice you leave the Estate this morning to meet someone in the woods? Now I'll ask you again Ophelia. What did you hear in the exchange between that evil woman and the Senator?'

Ariela watched Katerina carefully. Her aura was switching between blue and murky blue. She wasn't angry, she was afraid. She knew something was wrong but didn't understand exactly what. She also understood that the Healer was evil and that had to mean something positive.

'This is all my fault Mistress. I have friends amongst the Goth village where the Healer comes from. She is up to something and it isn't good. I've met with my friends and we have been keeping an eye on the Healer. Ophelia was just helping me.'

'So, what did you find out?' Katerina challenged Ophelia

'I…I didn't hear much but the Healer offered to supply the Senator with information about the village. I think she means to create conflict between the Romans and the Goths.'

'Why?' Katerina challenged again.

'She wants something the Senator keeps in his locked cupboard. Constantius showed it to me once. It's very precious.'

'How do I know this isn't an elaborate scheme you cooked up to steal that item for yourself? You and your friends could be thieves for all I know.' Katerina didn't seem to believe her own revelations but she was obviously still uncertain.

'I can't prove anything to you. I guess you will have to decide if you want to hand me over to the Senator or not.'

Katerina looked from Ophelia to Ariela and sighed. She released the servant girl and her shoulders sagged in resignation. Her eyes popped open wide as she suddenly thought of something. 'Where is Constantius anyway?'

'He is safe. He went mad from the drug the Healer has been giving him. My friends are looking after him.

He'll return later tonight once the drug is out of his system and I can sneak out and bring him back.'

'You'll go get him now girl, before the Senator starts asking after him. You too Ophelia. I don't know who to trust right now but I've known you since you were a little girl. You go where she goes and I'll see where my loyalties lie after Constantius is back.'

Ophelia curtsied and Ariela followed. 'Yes Mistress.' Both girls chimed in unison.

'Well don't just stand there. Get on your way.'

Chapter 18

'Culaan?' Ariela called out quietly as she made her way toward the cave entrance. 'It's me.'

Culaan stepped from the shadows, a wide grin on his lips as he scooped Ariela from her feet and wrapped her in his arms. 'What are you doing here? I wasn't expecting you until after dark.'

'It's a long story. We have so much to tell you. Is Constantius alright?'

Culaan lowered Ariela to the ground, his smile fading at the mention of the Roman nobleman. 'Yes,' was his short and rather curt reply. Ariela reached up and brushed his lips with hers.

'You have no right to be jealous you know! I've seen the trail of pretty woman who goggle at your every move and quiver at every smile you send their way. I still remember the night I first laid eyes on you, dancing in the moonlight with ladies on your arm, your drunken swagger not enough to deter any of them.'

'That is different.'

'How so?'

'I didn't care about any of them. You care about that sack in there. I know you do.'

'Yes, as I care about anyone mixed up in my world who doesn't deserve to be. You are going to have to learn to understand the difference between care and love.' Ariela placed her open palm on Culaan's bearded cheek. 'You are also going to have to lose that.' She tugged on his now long, rough whiskers.

'Ouch! I thought they made me look older, more distinguished.'

'You haven't been near a mirror lately then have you?' Ariela smiled to soften her words as she moved into the cave.

'Ariela! So good to see you, and Ophelia.' Genevieve looked up as both women walked in, followed by Culaan still rubbing his face.

The small fire offered a glow around the gloomy walls and Ariela could see her friend snuggled in the corner with Constantius as though they were long-lost friends. She looked from Genevieve and turned to Culaan, an obvious question in her eyes. He shrugged off any reply and Genevieve continued on as though nothing odd had occurred.

'We have some hare stew left. Did you want some? Why are you here so early?'

'We had a visitor today. The Healer came to the Estate and met with the Senator. Ophelia got caught eavesdropping and Katerina, the Mistress of the house pushed us both for answers. She sent us out here to bring Constantius back before the Senator gets curious.

'Alright but we need to do some back-tracking first. Genevieve has filled our young budding Emperor here in on his appalling behaviour.' Culaan paced as he spoke.

'I'm sorry for that by the way.' Constantius chimed in quietly from the shadows.

'We'll tell you what we have been doing and you can fill us in on what you've been doing. The Angel put us in different places for a reason, now we need to find out why.' Culaan crossed his arms and sat down on his haunches by the small fire.

'Well I found myself as a servant for the Senator, you know that. I met Ophelia here who is actually a Guardian of magical relics.'

'A what?' Constantius interrupted, suddenly lost amongst these strange newcomers.

'We'll give you more details soon Constantius but you remember how I tossed you across the Senator's study?' The nobleman nodded. 'Well there is a lot more to it that you don't really know yet. Let us share notes first and then we can answer your questions.'

The Emperor's son nodded his understanding but failed to relax with the knowledge.

'Anyway, the Healer...' Ariela carried on explaining.

'Andronica.' Culaan offered.

'Alright, Andronica is after a relic that can take us back in time or neutralise my powers or anyone as powerful as me. But if it can take us back in time, it can take her too. I'm not sure why she wants it, but she is pretty determined to get it.'

'That isn't good.' Genevieve joined the conversation. 'We've met her and she is a nasty one.

Short temper. Happy to hurt anyone who gets in her way.'

'Yes, and there is something else strange about her. She gives me the creeps but at the same time, I can't help but feel something familiar about her.' Culaan finally sat down, filling a bowl of stew as he spoke.

'I think that is because she comes from our time.' Ariela offered. 'I told you she visited me in spirit. I'm sure I felt Morrigan with me. Don't ask me how, across hundreds of years in time, but I am sure Andronica recognised her too.'

'What did she want from the Senator?' Constantius joined the conversation, his curiosity piqued.

'Well I think after we interrupted her plans to get Brísingamen through you, the Senator was the next best choice.'

'Brísingamen! That's the relic I showed you?'

'Yes.' Ariela took the bowl of stew Culaan offered her and watched as he poured another for Ophelia.

'From what Ophelia has gathered, Andronica plans to stir up trouble with the tribes, to give an excuse to provide information in exchange for the relic, or worse, to cause a distraction so she can steal it.' Ariela took a mouthful of her food and savoured the flavour.

'This is nicer than your cooking Ariela.' Ophelia laughed.

'I told you. I'm a Priestess, cooking isn't my gift.'

'That is an understatement.' Culaan laughed and Ariela slapped him on the arm playfully.

****

Andronica took her frilled blouse and long skirt off and replaced them with a simple long tunic. She wrapped her heavy woollen cape around her shoulders and rubbed the bone ring on her finger.

It had tingled the whole time she had been in the Senator's office. She was sure the young servant was listening in, but when she tried to read the girl's thoughts, there was nothing but jumbled stupid visions of that pretty wooden door she was cleaning.

Still, there was something not quite right about the Estate. The girl with the power was there, but not too close. She needed to spend more time studying the newcomers. Somehow, they were there to interfere with her plans, but she couldn't yet figure out how or why.

First, she needed to mend the bridge between herself and the tribe leader. Reznor was a strong man, well respected and she knew her fiery temper had gotten away from her earlier.

Andronica crossed the clearing in front of her cabin and made her way over toward the main meeting area. There was a small group of tall trees in the middle of a large expansive common area. The outer edge was rimmed with spring time flowers and little homes dotted the cleared area in front of the forest.

Reznor drew his bow and loosened a shaft into the target before him. His son Blaze clapped excitedly as the arrow found its mark right in the centre of the red dot on the straw dummy's chest.

'Kill shot Atta!'

'Your turn Blaze.'

The boy had a bow half the size of his father's but it still took strength to draw the full power. Blaze took a breath, held it while he took aim and released his breath before he released the shaft. The arrow flew quickly across the clearing, slamming into the chest of the dummy, a hand's space to the left of his father's shot.

'Good, now adjust your aim to suit. Did you allow for wind drift? It isn't much, but there is a little wind from the East.'

Reznor saw the Healer approaching and he was in no mood to expose Blaze to her foul temper. He watched the boy release the next shaft, which landed slightly to the right of his own perfect shot. 'Nicely done Blaze. You keep practising now. I have to meet with someone.'

Blaze didn't take his eyes from the target. Instead he reached into his quiver and notched another arrow, lining up for another attempt to slice his father's arrow in half.

'He'll be a better archer than you Reznor.' Andronica offered as the chief drew within earshot.

'You'll not soften me up this day Andronica. Your little display earlier left a foul taste in my mouth.'

'And so it should have. I apologise. I only have the best interests of the tribe at heart. You have strangers in your midst whom you trust more than your own Healer.'

'They have given me no cause for mistrust.'

Andronica could see she wasn't making the headway she had hoped for. Reznor was no-one's fool.

'Just be wary Reznor. That boy of yours deserves a chance to rule his people. I've seen the girl Thor speaks

of. She is a servant in the Senator's household. Maybe
they are spies sent by the Romans?'

Reznor watched the woman before him. 'How is it
you have seen her?'

Andronica smiled in a way that looked more like a
sneer. 'You are too clever for your own good Reznor.'

'Thank you for you counsel Healer, but I have
men for that. Your work here is to heal injuries and if that
is outside your scope of interest now — if we are boring
you — then you are free to return to whichever people
you came to us from.'

'Is that a dismissal?' Andronica felt her amulet
hum and the ring on her finger tingled in response to her
rise in emotion. She wanted to release her powers, but
now was not the time. She took a deep breath to compose
herself.

'Of course not. But we have no intention of
keeping you here if you have a better place to be.' Reznor
nodded his head and made it clear the conversation had
come to an end.

Andronica bit her lip to contain her retort and
watched as the King of the Goths turned his back on her
with disregard.

Chapter 19

'Oh thank goodness you found him.' Katerina looked relieved as the two serving girls returned to the Estate with Constantius. 'Are you well my lord?'

'I'm fine thank you Mistress. These two servants have helped me through a difficult illness. I think I should rest though. I will speak with the Senator in the morning. Can you advise him I've returned and apologise on my behalf?'

'Of course. He was all set to send out a search party, assuming the Goths had captured you for ransom or something worse.'

'Even more reason you advise him as soon as possible. I wouldn't want the villagers to be held responsible for my lack of communication.'

Constantius turned and made his way up the stairs without another word. Katerina frowned at his back and scowled at the girls who tried not to giggle at her false show of concern. Her lack of love for Constantius was already well established.

'Alright, now tell me if you managed to inform your friends about the village Healer?'

'We did. They should have the situation under control, but I'd like to pay a visit this evening if you don't mind?' Ariela ventured.

'You need to get some rest girl. You also need to be seen in the actual Estate or the other servants will start to ask questions.' Katerina protested.

'You can smooth them over. You give the orders. It is really important I keep an eye on Andronica. She is very powerful.'

'Powerful? What on earth do you mean?'

Ariela suddenly remembered that Katerina didn't know about her magic or Andronica's. 'She holds a huge sway with the village leaders and if she tells them the Senator is out for their blood, they are likely to believe her. We want to avoid a war between the tribes and Rome, don't we?' Ariela searched Katerina's face for confirmation.

'Very well. You go, but leave Ophelia here. She has plenty of her own chores to catch up on and can more easily cover for your absence.'

Both girls nodded and rushed to the cookhouse. It had been a long day and they were hungry again. Ariela cut a large chunk of cheese, while Ophelia found some fresh bread and dried fruit. They washed the meal down with fresh orange juice and water.

'You need to keep an eye on Brísingamen. For all we know the Senator is already set to hand it over. Constantius will make sure it's secure in the morning, when he can get into the Senator's study, but anything could happen tonight.

Ophelia nodded her understanding. 'You be careful. Do you really need to go to the village? Can't your friends handle it? Genevieve seems pretty capable to me and so does Culaan.'

'Yes, but neither of them can wield magic like I can and if Andronica has planned some sort of upset between the tribes and the Romans then she may unleash some magic in the process. I'm also not convinced Culaan and Genevieve have the full support of the Goths. Andronica has been with them for some time and a village Healer holds a lot of sway.'

'You are right. I'll watch Brísingamen.'

'I'm curious though. I've been thinking about something. You said Brísingamen didn't become visible again until Constantius took it out of the cupboard. If you weren't warding the cupboard to protect Brísingamen from sight, who was?'

Ophelia frowned and pulled at her ear absently. 'I have no idea!'

****

Ariela couldn't risk being seen taking a horse. It was going to be a long walk to the village without one but she couldn't transport her physical self, only her spirit. Yet in spirit, she was of little use to Culaan if he needed her.

The young Priestess considered her options. She could drug the guards and take a horse, but that would be noticed. She suddenly remembered the night Andronica had come to the Estate. She had only travelled in spirit a short distance, so she had entered the grounds unseen.

'How on earth did you pass the guards unnoticed?' Ariela found a quiet place in the garden, hidden behind the dormitory in the late afternoon sun. She closed her eyes and focussed her energy on all the rituals she had learned from such an early age. The thoughts of her mother and father raised painful, yet joyful memories and the Priestess suppressed them to find what she really needed.

'That's what I want. A concealing spell.' It was magic and forbidden by the Order, but the Egyptian witch Jezebel had taught it to the class in order that they would recognise it when they felt it. Someone using the spell would create a flow of air unseen by the eye, but felt by the senses.

Ariela went over the spell in her mind, one step at a time. There would have been a moment not so long ago when she would have shuddered at the idea of using magic, but that time was past. The Angel had brought her here, with all her knowledge and experience to do what she was trained to do. Guilt was useless and this was important.

The Priestess felt for the molecules of moisture in the air. She folded them and layered them until she could no longer see her own hand. She smiled triumphantly. 'Now, can I do the same to a horse?' She asked as she made her way to the barn.

Chapter 20

Culaan and Genevieve returned to the village as the evening shadows grew long. The village was in the midst of a celebration and the two warriors looked at each other in confusion.

'Did we miss our invitation?' Culaan asked.

'We must have. How could they forget to invite the gods?' Both laughed aloud as Blaze ran toward them, an excited look on his young face.

'You are here, finally. We have been waiting.'

'For us?' Culaan tapped his chest innocently.

'It's a feast in your honour.' Blaze took Culaan by the hand before realising what he was doing. 'Oh, sorry. Is it allowed? To touch a god?'

Culaan laughed. 'Of course. Tell me, what has brought this on?'

'You'll have to ask Atta.'

Culaan followed Blaze into the main village square. The homes were illuminated with torches, the fragrance of flowers filling the senses. There was a large boar roasting on an enormous fire to the North of the clearing, right in front of Reznor's home.

The music floated on the air as the sun dipped slowly behind the mountains.

'I wish Ariela could be here.' Culaan whispered to Genevieve over his shoulder.

Genevieve shrugged without answering and scanned the crowd for Griffin. She spotted him alongside Reznor and waited for him to notice her. A smile crept across his face as they approached.

'Blaze said this celebration is for us?' Culaan enquired.

'Well in a way it is. We've heard some rumours the Romans are planning on dispersing our village and others in order to gain more control over our people. You said you would support us if the time came. It looks like this might be a pre-war dinner.'

Culaan stood silently taking in the new information. He rubbed his chin and suddenly remembered he was supposed to shave off his beard. He smiled at the thought before bringing his focus back to Reznor.

'Well that is interesting. I just met with someone from the Senator's Estate today. Our friend who was missing is no longer missing. Let's just say it is the work of the gods, but we have much to discuss. Can we talk somewhere privately?'

'After the ceremony?'

'Ceremony?'

'Yes.' Reznor smiled. 'Don't the gods need a sacrifice before battle?'

Culaan felt a little uneasy, but he didn't flinch. 'Well generally that is customary. What did you have in mind?'

'Well let's first have a little fighting exhibition, then we'll attend to the sacrifice.'

'Fighting exhibition? We've been through this.'

'Yes, but we thought god against god would be more enjoyable to see. You can't actually kill each other, can you?'

Culaan scanned the assembly. There were mugs of ale being raised in unanimous agreement with the chief and the Celtic warrior turned slowly to take in the entire village for the first time.

The last hint of daylight shone across the clearing toward the Healer's cottage and Andronica stood with her robe wrapped around her shoulders, a thin unwelcoming smile upon her lips. *This is your doing!*

Culaan leant forward to whisper, but Griffin stepped between him and the Chief. Culaan spoke anyway, just loudly enough for both men to hear. 'Well I had come to tell you the spy in your midst wasn't me, but if I have to fight to prove it, we can do that.'

Culaan turned to Genevieve and questioned her with his eyes. She smiled mischievously and nodded her agreement.

Both warriors prepared. It wasn't the first time they had sparred and they could do so without inflicting fatal injury but at what point would Reznor consider the exhibition over?

Genevieve took a leather tie from her pocket and drew her hair up into a high ponytail, revealing a small red birthmark. Culaan took his heavy woollen shirt off and threw it into the crowd. Oohs and aahs accompanied the sight of his exposed chest and Reznor chuckled at the brazen, confident behaviour.

Andronica moved closer to get a better view. She had planned to instil mistrust in Reznor's opinion of the newcomers, but this was more than she could have hoped for. As she found a place on a sawn log, she noticed Genevieve's neck. Her blood ran cold like the thawed mountain frost and she almost stopped the fight immediately.

It isn't possible. It can't be. If she is, then he is. Oh what have I done?'

There was nothing she could do now. If she interrupted, all her plans would be for nothing. Reznor needed to test these two, but now she was worried. She didn't want either of them to be hurt.

Chapter 21

Culaan circled Genevieve, his staff twirling in the torch light of the makeshift arena.

The strike of wood on wood rang out loudly around the village square as soft murmurs surrounded the combatants.

Genevieve made the first strike, hitting Culaan on his left shoulder and following through with a jab to his stomach. He grunted softly at the impact.

'You don't have to hit so hard you know.'

'Really? I think we had better make the show believable. Aren't you the least bit curious why they want us to fight?'

Culaan shrugged. 'We could ask them if you like!'

Genevieve looked from Culaan to Reznor and then at Griffin. 'I think you should.'

Culaan was growing frustrated with the situation. 'Reznor. What is this ceremony really all about?'

'It's a test.'

Andronica saw her opening. Her chance to stop the fight. 'It is a test you don't need to complete.'

'Really?' Reznor rose from his chair. 'That seems to be fine words coming from you.'

'What do you mean?' Andronica made her way from her seat and out into the light of the arena.

'I have questions and I am going to get some answers. You've all been lying to me.' Reznor waved his hand and Griffin moved out of sight for only a moment. When he returned, an unconscious woman with dark hair and bronze skin was being dragged between two large tribesmen. Her hair hung over her lolling head, her bare feet slid along the dirt, her dress tattered and torn.

'No!' Culaan reached for his sword, suddenly realising he was unarmed. 'Clever.' His smile did not reach his eyes as he understood now why the farce of staff fighting was Reznor's choice.

'You bastard.' Genevieve spun her only weapon threateningly. 'We had news for you. We offered to help you and you repay us with deceit and attacks on one of our friends?'

'*You* speak of deceit. Griffin saw her,' Reznor pointed to Andronica 'meeting with the Senator.'

'That has nothing to do with us and everything to do with what we wanted to tell you.' Culaan protested.

'Possibly true, but your friend here, she was seen returning to the Estate with the Roman Emperor's son. They looked very comfortable together. You said you hated the Romans. Are you a spy? Is *she* a spy?' Reznor pointed to the unconscious Ariela.

'When she wakes up, you are going to know more than the wrath of Thor. You are going to wish you took the time to listen to us.' Griffin lifted Ariela's head by her hair. Her face was bruised and Culaan almost lunged at Griffin as Genevieve growled at the sight of her friend.

'I thought the Romans were barbaric.' Culaan spoke as he saw Ariela begin to stir. 'We wanted to warn you that the Romans possess a powerful relic and Andronica is seeking it. We tried to tell you all of this in confidence, but you are more of a fool than I thought.' Culaan moved forward, this time Griffin failed to stop him. 'We are sent by the gods, or God or the angels. I honestly don't really know, but we came here to stop that woman from getting her hands on any more powerful weapons.'

Culaan pointed at Andronica, drawing attention away from Ariela. He needed to give her time, but he could see his words were starting to sink in. Reznor looked from Culaan to Andronica who looked more nervous than he had ever seen her.

The energy release came without warning to everyone but Culaan. Ariela's two assailants were thrown sideways, landing heavily enough to knock them unconscious.

Culaan ran to her, barely reaching her in time to prevent her from falling to the ground. 'What happened?' He touched her cheek.

'I don't know.' She breathed heavily, struggling to regain her vision.

A haze of smoke rose from the arena. The visibility was reduced so much, Culaan could hardly see Ariela in his arms. He lifted her from the ground, hugging her protectively. 'Genevieve?' He called into the thick fog as he carefully moved toward where he had last seen her.

Men were rushing around trying to find the cause of the smoke. 'Someone put that fire out.' Reznor bellowed.

'There is no fire.' Griffin called out from the centre of the arena.

'What is going on? How did she throw those men aside like chaff?' Reznor demanded to anyone who would answer him.

'We owe you *no* explanation!' Culaan tried to control his anger. He could no longer see Reznor, but he shouted at him in any case.

'I'm alright, you can put me down now.' Ariela touched Culaan on the cheek as he lowered her carefully to her feet.

Ariela waved her hands gently through the air, forcing the smoke haze to clear. 'It was Andronica. I felt her power surge.'

Culaan looked around the clearing. 'Where is Genevieve? What have you done with her?' The accusations were clear as he made eye-contact with Reznor once more.

'It wasn't Reznor, Culaan. I think Andronica has her.'

Chapter 22

'First Reznor, now you. What is going on?'
Genevieve squirmed in her restraints and shook her head
trying to clear her mind. The last thing she remembered
was the smoky haze in the arena and after that,
everything went black.

'I want to let you go but I have a few questions
first. I don't want to hurt you.'

'Why don't I believe you.' Genevieve screwed up
her nose as though she had smelt a foul odour.

'Where did you get that birthmark?' Andronica
moved closer to Genevieve but maintained a safe
distance. The Huntress sat on her haunches, ready to
spring into action at any moment.

'Now that is a stupid question. It's a *birth*mark.'
Genevieve pulled more vigorously at her bindings.

'It's difficult to explain.' Andronica seemed
uncharacteristically uncomfortable.

'No, really! You knocked me out with some sort of
powder and now you have me tied up in,' Genevieve
suddenly looked around trying to make out her
surroundings, 'who knows where. Of course, it's hard to
explain. You are insane.'

'No, no I'm quite sane. This is going to be hard for you to believe so let me tell you a few things that might help you understand I'm telling the truth.'

'I'd rather you just let me go so I can kick your butt and return to my friends.' Genevieve continued to look for anything that she could use for a weapon or a means of escape. The location wasn't familiar. The room seemed to be similar to the cave they had stayed in the night before, but it wasn't the same place.

The walls were damp as though they were underground. Genevieve felt the ground below her feet and realised it was solid rock as she suspected, yet the roof of the room was lined with rafters, as though another storey stood above them.

Andronica began to speak and Genevieve returned her attention to the Healer. 'I don't know exactly how you got here, probably in a similar way to me, but I'm going to go out on a limb and say you came from a small village in Galatia where the wise woman was known as Morrigan?'

Genevieve opened her mouth to speak but no words came out. She finally composed herself and looked the woman in the eye, carefully trying to gauge her. 'Someone must have told you.' She licked her lips with a nervousness that was seeping into her soul.

'Who? Your friends aren't exactly on speaking terms with me. While we are talking, who is your friend? I'd like to bet his father is Owyn?'

'Now you are just getting creepy.'

'So, his father is Owyn then? I don't believe it.'
Andronica sat heavily on a rough wooden bench that ran
along the wall opposite Genevieve.

'Don't believe what?' The Huntress squinted in the
dim light to make out the Healer's expression. She
seemed genuinely shocked but Genevieve reminded
herself not to be foolish.

'Your real name is Genevieve, right?' She watched
the girl before her carefully, a sudden emotion crossed
her face, 'and your brother is Culaan.'

'Who are you? Culaan is not my brother.'
Genevieve felt suddenly ill. She loved Culaan, more than
she could ever tell anyone, but she had never been able to
have anything more than a strong friendship with him.

'Yes, your brother is Culaan. Search your heart,
you know he is.'

'You're mad, we've been friends our entire life.'
Genevieve suddenly felt close to tears. 'What magic are
you using on me woman? Stop it!'

'I'm not using magic Genevieve.' Andronica
moved closer. 'You may have heard my name spoken in
quiet adult conversations between Morrigan and Owyn.
Maybe not. They called me Andraste and I'm your
mother Genevieve, and Culaan's.'

Genevieve stared uncomprehendingly for a long
moment. Her mind raced with realisation. 'You were
banished! Culaan's mother was a powerful druid, exiled
for... I don't really know what for, but Culaan is not my
brother. You are not my mother.'

'I am. If Morrigan were here even she could not
deny it. Owyn knew nothing of you. I gave you to

Morrigan to keep you safe. She kept your parentage secret to protect you.'

'Protect me from what, who?'

'From Owyn. He hated me after I left. He found out I was with child and wanted the baby. We gave him Culaan, but we couldn't give him you. He would have assumed you carried my powers. I wasn't sure what he might do.'

'Why? Culaan could just as easily have been a Druid as me?'

'No child. When you were born, you were marked.'

'What, this little red dot?' Genevieve fingered her birthmark.

'Yes.' The Druid lifted her hair and showed an identical mark on her own neck. 'Owyn was in no state to assume the best of you, so Morrigan agreed to keep your existence secret.'

'She tried to yell something to us when we left. That must have been it.' Genevieve shook her head to clear her thoughts. 'None of that matters. You have been wreaking havoc. You have endangered Culaan and myself, Ariela and her friend. You drugged Constantius just to steal the relic, to get more power. Isn't that why you were exiled to begin with?' The Huntress had no idea why she posed the statement as a question, but she did and Andraste wasn't letting the opportunity slip by.

'I was exiled because Owyn discovered how old I was and that I had been involved in the treaty that enslaved the Galatian tribes to the Romans. That is why I want the relic. I aim to return and undo what I did. I've spent the last few hundred years traveling forward in time, collecting the objects of power to help me bring the Druids back. I finally have a chance to go back, but I need Brísingamen to do that. Help me Genevieve. Help me restore the power our people deserve. Help me destroy the Roman Empire before it begins.'

Chapter 23

'It seems we have a common enemy.' Reznor approached Culaan carefully, aware that even if he weren't the god Thor, he, or the girl with him held power of some sort.

'I could have told you that if you had bothered to listen, before all this commotion.' Culaan puffed his chest and clenched his fists, obviously fighting for control. 'Where would she take her?' Culaan growled.

'I have no idea. The Healer has been a mystery from the moment she arrived, but she has served the village well. She warned us you were up to something. Griffin reported what he had seen. I'm sorry I tested you.'

'I'm not Thor. I know you had your doubts but we *were* sent here by the gods. No matter which way we describe it, you'll find it hard to believe.' Culaan spoke quietly, barely above a whisper.

'Let's leave the clearing.' The villagers were dispersing after the smoke haze had lifted and Reznor felt no need to frighten his people with talk of the disappearance of the woman they considered to be the goddess Skathi.

'I found some tracks.' Griffin joined Reznor as the small group made their way inside Reznor's cottage. Culaan helped steady Ariela with one hand as she mounted the porch steps.

'Good, where is she heading?' Reznor moved inside the musty smelling main room. The hint of wood-fire smoke hung in the air. 'Blaze, fetch us some water and ale boy.' The chief's son came out of his hiding place with a wide grin on his face.

'Oh Atta, how did you know I was here?'

'Because you are always where you shouldn't be Blaze.' Reznor grinned and tussled the boy's curly blonde locks as he darted outside to fill a jug of water from the well and fetch some ale from the storeroom.

'He's a fine boy.' Culaan remarked as the front door slammed shut behind him.

'Yes, and I don't want to break his heart with the truth of who you really are.'

'I am the son of a Galatian Celtic Chieftain named Owyn. My mother was a Druid and that is where I am told my power over the magical sword comes from.

Genevieve is my best friend. We grew up together and this is Ariela, Priestess of the Order of Shiloh, formed by her mother, Nina, first Priestess of the Order in the times of Israel.'

'Well! The Galatian tribes migrated north a few centuries ago and the Israelites, well let's just say you're a long way from home girl.' Reznor directed his remark to Ariela who had sat quietly taking in their situation.

'You seem not to be a believer Reznor?'

Reznor shrugged, 'I've seen a lot in my short time as Chieftain of the Visigoths but other than Andronica's remarkable healing abilities and your little show of strength earlier with my men, I haven't seen anything that would support your claim. I'm happy to maintain a little heathy scepticism.'

Ariela swirled her right hand above her head. 'I understand now why faith is such a hard concept. You always have to see it for yourselves to believe.' The glow grew slowly at first, until the room was suddenly alight with the golden orb sitting in the palm of the Priestess's hand.

Griffin backed up so fast he flipped the stool he had been sitting on out from underneath himself. His sword was drawn before he could breathe. Ariela flicked her other hand at the warrior and a burst of air flung him gently off his feet onto his buttocks, a loud grunt exploded with the air from his lungs as he landed heavily.

'I'm not a god, or a goddess, but there are those who possess the same power as I have and have not the moral compass to know how and when to use it. They, like Andronica seem to think they can do whatever they want, defying God and his minions. That is why we are here.'

Griffin was back on his feet, sword raised for the assault, but Reznor calmly held his hand up for the young man to remain calm. 'How do we know you are of good moral judgement?'

'A good question. I guess you don't know, except that so far, surely our actions have not betrayed us.'

Ariela let the ball of light extinguish in her hands and
Griffin sheathed his sword, staying a good distance away
from the Priestess as he fumbled with his stool, moving it
to the far corner of the room to take a seat.

'Where did the tracks lead Griff?' Reznor decided
to change the subject.

'They went back to the Healer's cottage, but there
was no one inside.'

'Andronica may have cloaked herself somehow.
Do you mind if I take a look?' Ariela asked but was
already on her feet heading for the door when Blaze
came running through, jug in hand, hair flying behind
him.

'Be my guest.' Reznor rose to accompany the
Priestess, Culaan pushed between the Chieftain and
Ariela, shouldering the man gently out of his path with a
smile that was far from welcoming.

'I think she can protect herself my friend.' Reznor
smiled amicably.

'I was your friend, but I think that time has
passed.' Culaan nodded to Blaze as he left the cottage.

The boy frowned accusingly at his father for an
answer, but none came.

Chapter 24

'Look. I am going to untie you now. We need to get away from here. I need your help Genevieve.'

'I'm not sure I can believe what you've told me. Either way, going back in time isn't safe. Ariela said so.'

'How old is your friend Ariela?'

'I don't know exactly. A few years younger than me but she is a Priestess of an ancient Order.' Genevieve spoke as though she were drowsy. She wasn't tired but her mind was struggling to focus and make sense of her mother's revelations.

'Really, which Order?'

'Shiloh. The Priestesses of Shiloh were started by her mother. She has travelled through time before we joined her.' Genevieve frowned at her confession. What was happening to her? Why was she sharing so much about Ariela?

'Well I am over five hundred years on this earth. I've travelled through hundreds of years of history to be here now and I assure you, bringing the Druids back to power is the right thing to do.'

Genevieve nodded. She felt unsure, but this was her mother, her only connection to who she really was.

Morrigan had lied to her, her father may have killed her
if he had known of her and now Culaan would never
love her the way she had hoped he would and she felt
somehow violated by her own thoughts of him for all the
years she had longed for her own brother's touch.

'Where are we going?'

'I need to find a way to get Brísingamen.
Constantius is useless it seems, so if I can convince the
Senator to attack the Goths, then he will leave the Estate
long enough so that we can easily get access to the relic.
It is in a locked cupboard that has a protection over it. I
can't open it, but I think you probably can.'

'Why?' Genevieve held out her hands for
Andraste to untie her. The woman waved her hand and
the bindings fell away without a touch.

'I have a hunch, but I don't have time to explain.
We need to move, now. Your friends will find us soon
otherwise. Are you with me daughter?'

Genevieve nodded. The mention of her friends
confused her for only a moment. The sound of her
mother's voice, calling her daughter drove her to
abandon her past for a new future. She felt numb,
emotionless as she watched her mother move toward the
other end of the cave they were hiding in.

A dim light appeared above the Huntress and a
ladder that had been there all along suddenly appeared
with the flick of Andraste's fingers.

'How?' Genevieve asked as she started up the
ladder.

'I will show you how when we get a moment. You have the power; I can feel it in you. With training, you could be more powerful than your Priestess friend.'

The thought somehow sent tingles down Genevieve's spine. Why, she couldn't exactly say, but Ariela had everything she had ever wanted. Now was her chance to get some of what she had always desired for herself.

****

Ariela was the first one through the door of the Healer's cottage. It was sparsely furnished with a bed, built up on a wooden box, a table, two chairs, a wall of shelving full of scrolls and jars of herbs and a hearth, full of smouldering wood that created a soft glow in the darkness.

'Is she here still?' Culaan moved up alongside and Ariela and searched her face for any clue. 'Can you sense her? Is Genie here?'

Ariela took Culaan's hand and steadied herself. She closed her eyes and allowed her spirit to seek out any power, any essence of Andronica or Genevieve. 'They have gone.'

'How? We've had a man on the door since I found the tracks!' Griffin protested and began lifting the mattress on the bed as though he might find two women hiding under the covers.

Ariela considered his words. 'If they couldn't leave by the front door, then Andronica must have another entry into this cottage.'

As if on cue, Griffin's search revealed a number of doors on the surface of the box that usually housed Andronica's mattress.

'Here, look at this.' There was a large door, with a small metal ring-pull handle on the top. Griffin lifted the handle to reveal a ladder that descended into the ground, but it was the smaller door that had Ariela's full attention. She could feel something, something unfamiliar, yet somehow familiar at the same time.

'Wait!' Ariela called as Griffin and Culaan almost fell over each other trying to see who could get down the ladder first.

Culaan turned at the tone of Ariela's voice. 'What's wrong?'

'I'm not sure. Look! There is another hidden compartment.' The Priestess opened the wooden door that came away in her hand. The opening wasn't large, but she could still easily reach inside.

'Be careful. I wouldn't be surprised if that woman left an adder or something just a vicious in that hiding hole.' Reznor nodded his agreement and all three men held their breath as the Priestess began her search.

The thought made Ariela hesitate only a moment, but she couldn't sense anything alive in the darkness. As she removed items, one by one, she marvelled at the collection. 'She must have been in an awful hurry to leave these behind.'

'Why take Genevieve and leave all this?' Culaan moved closer to study the contents. He saw a silver star with a blue stone in the centre. There was a wooden Egyptian Ankh, engraved with hieroglyphic symbols and rubbed with gold. He caught sight of what had to be a Celtic symbol, a three-sided star, knotted together with a circle intersecting it. But it was the last symbol Ariela removed that made her gasp. It was a circle, with the star of Israel in the centre, surrounded by alchemic symbols that represented water, earth, fire, sun, moon and more. It was made of bronze but it shone with a white light as the Priestess took it in her hand. When she put it down on the wooden bed box, the light dissipated.

The reaction had everyone mesmerized, and when Ariela touched it again, the light returned but this time with a hum that everyone could hear.

'What is that? Culaan looked up from the strange relic and into Ariela's tear-filled eyes. Her cheeks ran with tear stains, left behind in the soot of the earlier smoke haze.

'It was my mother's,' was all she could say.

Culaan reached out and took her in his arms. He knew she was momentarily overwhelmed but he needed to find Genevieve. As if reading his mind, Reznor spoke.

'Griff and I will head in first. You two follow as soon as you can. We'll see if there is any trail left inside to follow.'

Ariela looked at Griffin, already halfway down the hole into utter darkness. 'You'll need this. I'll be with you soon. I just need a moment to catch my breath.' She opened her palm to an orb of light, nowhere near as bright as the first ball of golden fire she created. This one pulsed with nothing stronger than the brightest candle.

Griffin looked at it with trepidation.

'It won't bite you Griff, take it. You'll see nothing without it down there. You want to find Genevieve, don't you?' Reznor knew he fancied the girl and the thought of finding her reassured him enough to take the orb in his hand.

Chapter 25

Ariela began to bundle the relics into a woollen scarf. She put her mother's Shiloh Order symbol away first, not wanting to dwell on it at that moment. The last relic in the pile gave her reason to pause.

'It can't be!' She breathed as Culaan looked up from the hidden doorway, already half way down through the opening.

'What is it?'

'I'm not sure. I need to investigate later.' She put the last relic with the Celtic star into the bundle and tied all four corners to make a small bundle. She tied another scarf to the tails of the bundle, making a shoulder strap and lifted it over her head and across her chest.

She took one last look around the room before following Culaan down into the darkness. Culaan drew his sword as he reached the ground below. The glow illuminated the room but Reznor and Griffin were both gone, the light of the orb shining from a doorway above, similar to the one they just came down at the far end of the hidden cave.

'How on earth did Andronica make this?' Culaan asked as he turned around, taking in the damp darkness and the false wooden floor above it.

'I am guessing it was always here, she just made sure to get Reznor to build her cottage here. She is a long way from the main village. That's relatively common for the Healer of the village. No one would have noticed her cutting the final hole into and out of the cave that was already here.'

'Oh, I was expecting some wild explanation about her magical powers forging an underground cave without making a sound.' Culaan seemed disappointed by the reality of the cave's construction.

Ariela laughed aloud at his boyish face in the light of his glowing sword.

'What do you think she wants with Genevieve?' He bit his lip as he finished his question.

'I really don't know. Maybe she thinks Genevieve can be held ransom for Brísingamen or maybe she wants to trade her for me? I'm the big threat as far as she is concerned.'

'Neither option sounds good to me. We had better catch up to Reznor and Griffin. Maybe they have found a clue to where they are going and how Andronica is keeping Genevieve under control.'

'Magic I would expect.' Ariela followed Culaan up the next ladder, leading out of the cave.

'Did you find anything?' Culaan asked as they caught up to Reznor and Griffin?

The second hidden door brought them out into the forest about a mile from the cottage. The area was dense with trees and undergrowth, the scent of pine and flowers floated on the still late-night air.

'We can't see the tracks in this light. We'll need to wait until dawn, then we'll track them and see where they ended up.' Reznor looked at Culaan as he spoke.

'I'm sorry I didn't trust you.'

Culaan shrugged. 'I'm not sure I would have trusted me if I were in your place. I just wish you had given us a chance to explain.'

'Me too.' Reznor agreed and Griffin nodded his accord, his worried expression creasing his already serious brow.

****

'Just tell the Senator what we agreed Genevieve and I will handle all the rest.' Andraste reassured her daughter. 'It will be alright. Once we have Brísingamen, we'll be able to go back to the beginning. You can stay with me. I won't have to leave either of you with Morrigan. I'll not leave you again, I promise.'

Genevieve stared ahead as they passed the guards on duty. They didn't move to stop either of them as they entered the Estate. Genevieve flexed her fingers and clenched her fists nervously as they made their way from the gates to the main foyer of the Senator's home.

She looked around the grand hall with the ornate stone spiral staircase that wounds its way up to the second storey. She expected to be challenged at any moment, having never experienced a welcoming arrival into any Roman stronghold.

The Mistress of the house greeted them politely, even at such an early hour and guided them up the stairs to the Senator's office. Genevieve allowed her fingers to glide along the stone railing. The material was cold and she supressed a shiver as it flowed down her spine.

She felt as though her mind was someplace else. She tried to focus on the large wooden door that the servant now knocked on, but somewhere in the back of her mind she felt as though she was missing something very important.

The thought disappeared as the dark wooden door swung open and she was ushered inside with her mother. She didn't know why, but she knew she should feel indignant about being ordered around, but no matter how much she tried, she simply found herself following along with her mother's plans. She felt like an insecure child, something she hadn't felt since she first realised she was an orphan.

'Always a pleasure to see you Andronica, but why so early? And who is your friend?' The Senator's expression changed as he took in the sight of Genevieve. Her bow remained slung over her shoulder, her hunting knife tied to her thigh. Her lean body spoke of her training and the Huntress couldn't decide if he was surprised or alert, but his posture had gone from slightly bored to attentive.

'This is my daughter, Genevieve. She is here with me to provide you with some important information. The early hour was necessary, it's a matter of urgency.'

'Really!' The Senator ushered the women to a lounge that sat in the corner of his study. There was a low stone table and a high-backed chair to one side. He took the chair as the women both sat. 'I didn't know you had a daughter.'

'She has been helping me discover what the Visigoth tribe have planned. You do remember I told you they were planning a revolt of some sort, don't you?'

'Of course I remember, but I've visited all my other spies and sources of information. Apart from some strange talk of the resurrection of their archaic gods, there has been nothing else. No talk of revolt. No one has refused to help with the mercenary army. Nothing odd at all.'

'Well that is just it. The gods you have heard them speak of, apparently, they *are* real, or at least someone has arrived in the village claiming to be Thor. I saw him with my own eyes, Genevieve too—you tell him dear.'

Genevieve looked from her mother to the Senator. There was something screaming at her in the back of her mind, but she couldn't hear it. She nodded her agreement as Andraste carried on.

'They claim that the Empire is stamping out their heritage, their culture and religion.'

'We've never asked them to put their beliefs aside. Why all this now?'

'They claim there is a prophecy, that the new religion the Emperor has adopted will grow so strong that the Emperor's son will try to stamp out the pagan religions of their people.'

'Nonsense.'

Andronica shrugged. 'I'm just telling you what they think. This Thor has come to rally them against Rome before it's too late.'

'I'll ride to the village and talk with Reznor. I'm sure we can settle this amicably. He's always been a reasonable man.'

'No! The god Thor, whether he is a god or not, has power, great power. I've seen it. His sword glows,' Genevieve frowned at her mother. Why was she trying to get Culaan killed? 'and there is a girl with them. She's been working as a spy on your own Estate. She is a weaver of magic.'

'You don't really believe in all that horse-dung do you?' The Senator looked at Andronica like she had gone insane, with a mix of surprise and pity.

'I've seen the glowing sword and the girl throws fire balls. You'll have to send the army in before they realise you're coming — otherwise they will have no chance — surprise is all you have.'

Chapter 26

Ophelia held her hand over her mouth for fear she might make a noise involuntarily. She moved away from the door and lifted her skirt high so as not to trip herself on the way down the stairs.

As she rounded the corner into the cookhouse, she bumped into Constantius. 'Oh my lord. I am sorry. Are you alright?'

'Thank you for your help Andronica and lovely to meet you Genevieve.' Ophelia could hear the conversation floating down the stairs and she pushed Constantius into the cookhouse with more force than she intended.

'What is going on?' The young noble spoke rather loudly and Ophelia shushed him with a finger on his lips. His eyes grew wide with mild outrage, but he allowed the servant to move him back toward the hearth and the long wooden preparation table.

'Be quiet! Ariela's life might depend on it.' That was all she could get out before Andronica moved past the entrance to the cookhouse. She stopped momentarily, as though she knew Ophelia had been eavesdropping, but the young Guardian shook her head back to reality. That had to be impossible, didn't it?

'Is that Genevieve with her?' Constantius whispered and Ophelia nodded vigorously. He made to move toward his new friend, but Ophelia grabbed his arm and shook her head with a frown that made the young noble stop without further protest.

The two women in the foyer moved on as Katerina led them out of the Senator's home. Ophelia waited until she heard the double wooden doors close firmly before she took a gulp of air and almost collapsed on the preparation table.

'We have to find Ariela, now!

'Why? What is going on? Why is Genevieve with the Healer?'

'I have no idea. She looked fine, unhurt, but she said nothing while Andronica told the Senator all sorts of lies; lies about your father, about a prophecy involving you, about Culaan and Ariela.'

'Wait. What prophecy?'

'Don't worry, I'm sure she just made it all up. We have to find Ariela. If she returns here, the Senator will arrest her.'

'Good luck with that is all I say. She is scary when she is angry. I wouldn't worry about her if I were you.' Constantius almost laughed as he recalled the few times he had tried to detain the Priestess.

'That may be the case, but either way, we need to warn her and the village that the Senator is sending the Centurions. They will be under attack in no time.'

'Under attack, why? They are allies, mercenaries that serve in our army.'

'True, but you do lord it over them quite a bit and that is beside the point. They aren't actually planning a mutiny, well not that I know of anyway.'

'So you think Andronica made it up? Why?'

'To keep the Senator busy I expect.'

'Why?'

'She wants Brísingamen to enhance her magic. You can't get it for her now, so the Senator is the next likely fool.'

'Fool?'

'I don't have time to explain, but I can't leave Brísingamen unguarded just in case. Can you go find Ariela?' Ophelia begged, knowing she was doing so to the future Emperor of Rome didn't seem to matter right now. This was too important. 'You know Andronica is after the relic? You were a little out of sorts when we talked about it in the cave. So, to make things brief, if she gets her hands on Brísingamen, then there is a really good chance your Empire might cease to exist. Is that reason enough to help me?'

Constantius considered the servant before him. He'd known her for quite a few years now and she had never shown any signs of delirium or over-reaction. 'If Rome is in danger, and so too Ariela and Genevieve, then I'll do what I can, but where should I start?'

'You can't exactly stroll into the village, if Andronica is back there, then that will be bad, but maybe follow her. See where she is taking Genevieve and see

what she is going to do next. Hopefully you'll find Ariela. I'm sure she will be looking for Andronica too.
****

'I don't understand!' Culaan watched Genevieve walk calmly from the Senator's Estate. She spoke quietly to Andronica as though nothing was out of order and it took all his strength to not call out to his lifelong friend.

'I told you, it's likely magic.' Ariela assured him, but as she watched Genevieve she wasn't so sure. Her eyes were relatively alert, not in the Huntress's usual manner, but they were not glazed over.

Griffin had begun tracking Andronica at first light and no one was surprised, least of all him to discover the Healer back at the Senator's Estate. They had waited for nearly an hour and all four were hungry and short on patience.

'We need to follow and see where they go.' Culaan moved to leave but Ariela grabbed him gently on the arm.

'No, we need to go in there and find out what Andronica was doing at the Estate. I'm sure Ophelia has been keeping an eye out.'

'Well we aren't exactly honoured guests in the Senator's home, being lowly mercenaries and all. What do you suggest we do?'

It was the first sign that Reznor was even remotely interested in taking Culaan or Ariela's lead, but it was a start.

'Best you return to the village. If Andronica goes back and you aren't there, she is likely to use her position with your people to her advantage.' Culaan looked to

Ariela to see if she agreed. The Priestess nodded and let go of his arm reluctantly.

'Sounds reasonable. Griffin, you follow them, I don't want any more surprises.' Reznor nodded to Griffin and both men rose carefully from the undergrowth.

'That's a good idea, but keep your distance. She is powerful, more powerful than you have seen and Reznor, don't ask me why I know, but she is planning something big, have your men prepared for anything.' Ariela offered as she returned her attention to the Estate.

'Culaan, follow me.' She led the warrior around the perimeter of the Estate, staying just inside the treeline, out of sight of the guards.

'You do know I've already snuck inside here to see you once.' Culaan smiled as Ariela scowled at him.

'You didn't sneak in, you waited for me outside in the forest. I want you behind me, not in front of me in case I need to protect you.'

'Protect me!'

Ariela smiled at the expected reaction.

'Baiting me again.'

'And you took it like true game.'

'I'm worried about Genie.' Culaan offered as they made their way to the rear entrance.

'Me too, but we need to focus on Brísingamen for the moment. Andronica may already have it. I need to find Ophelia and make sure she is alright. I hope she knows something.'

Culaan grabbed Ariela by the arm and pulled her back deeper into the undergrowth as the sound of footsteps finally reached her ears.

'How did you hear that?' She mouthed, Culaan answered with a condescending smile.

He let go of her arm and moved with lightning speed from their concealment, returning with a thrashing body, his mouth clamped shut with Culaan's hand. Ariela tried not to laugh as she looked upon Constantius's wide-eyed expression. The thrashing stopped as Ariela placed a finger on her lips, signalling the need for his silence. The young nobleman nodded and Culaan gently removed his hand.

'What are you doing out here?' Culaan asked rather more harshly than he had planned.

'Same question for you. I'm following Andronica and Genevieve.'

'We were too until we found they had visited here.' Ariela moved closer to Constantius and Culaan frowned at the proximity of her body to the Roman's.

She rolled her eyes and continued. 'Is Ophelia inside, does she know why Andronica visited?'

'She does and she told me if I ran into you to tell you not to go to the Estate. The Healer said something to the Senator that made it not safe for you to return. She didn't explain it all to me though.'

'Well we need to know exactly what Ophelia knows. Go back in there and tell her to come out here.'

'I'm not your servant! You're mine, remember.' Constantius was flustered and confused. 'She told me to follow Andronica. She said the fate of Rome was depending on it.'

'We have someone doing that. Just go back and ask Ophelia to come out and see me.' Ariela insisted.

'She won't leave. She said she is guarding Brísingamen. I don't understand all this. I thought Rome was complicated. I thought a sabbatical in the country would be a good idea.'

'Oh stop your whining will you. This is much bigger than you, bigger than even Rome. If Andronica gets what she wants, we might all be in trouble.'

'Ophelia said something similar. Look, I'll go get her but then I'm going back to my room. You can keep all this drama for yourselves.'

'That's an excellent idea.' Culaan interjected as Constantius started out of the undergrowth and back to the servant's entrance to the Estate.

Constantius, turned at the warrior's comment and frowned. He wasn't sure if he heard sarcasm in the man's voice, but either way, he knew he was supposed to be offended.

Chapter 27

The sound of marching feet and thundering hooves caused Ariela and Culaan to peer through the undergrowth. They struggled to get a clear vision but it wasn't hard to see there must have been a full legion of Roman Centurions and Legionaries approaching the Senator's Estate. The Centurion Primus dismounted his tall white stallion, removed his plumed helmet and strode purposefully toward the front entrance, past the guards who saluted him and on into the house.

'That isn't good,' Culaan whispered.

'That is the least of our worries.' Ophelia entered the thicker foliage and collapsed to the ground, her heart in her throat, her expression bleak.

'Ophelia. Thank God you're alright. I was worried about you.' Ariela joined her friend on the ground, embracing her with obvious relief.

'Andronica has told the Senator that you both lead the Goths against Rome and she even manufactured a prophecy about Constantius and his father bringing the new religion to Rome and threatening any Goth who follows their old ways.'

'Wow, that is extreme. There's nothing to support such a prophecy, is there?'

'Well, I honestly don't know. It's the first I've ever heard of it.'

'Problem for another day.' Culaan interrupted. 'Find Genie, get her away from Andronica and keep Brísingamen out of her hot little hands. That's the quest right?'

'Well for now, yes.' Ariela agreed.

'Look, I don't know how to tell you this, but Genevieve seemed to be helping Andronica willingly.' Ophelia was wringing her hands as she explained what she had seen.

'I hope you're wrong, but if Andronica hasn't used magic on her, why else would she be helping her? Ariela looked to Culaan for an explanation but none was forthcoming. He shrugged, a sad look in his eyes.

'Let's focus on them — the soldiers, why are they here?' Ariela looked back to Ophelia for more information.

'They are here to attack the Goth village.'

'We have to warn Reznor!' Culaan jumped to his feet. 'There are innocent people in the village! Blaze, everyone is at risk.'

'Yes, but we have to stay here and guard Brísingamen. This is exactly what she is planning, a diversion.' Ariela protested.

'How can we help Reznor and guard the Brísingamen at the same time?'

'I've got an idea, but I'll need to find a safe place.' Ariela offered.

'I think I can get you into the Estate. Follow me.' Ophelia moved carefully through the forest toward the back gate of the Estate.

'How do we get past the guard?' Culaan queried Ophelia as they surveyed the smaller stone entrance, with a narrow gateway used mostly by the servants.

'Give me a few minutes. I'll distract the guard. It won't be for long, but long enough to give you time to make it into the dormitory.'

'Where is Katerina? Will she see us and will she alert the guards if she does?' Ariela whispered as Ophelia rose to leave their hiding place.

'She will be busy with the Senator and the Centurion Primus. They will be meeting in the Senator's study. Either way, she's been helpful so far, I don't see her putting us in the executioner's hands anytime soon.'

'Alright, don't take too long. We really don't need to get caught out in the open like this.' Culaan looked calmer than he felt.

'What! Surely you are looking for any excuse to use that pretty glowing sword of yours!' Ophelia smiled as Culaan scowled in reply.

****

Culaan sat on the edge of the bed as Ariela laid down to make herself more comfortable. 'You'll need to stay alert Culaan. My body is vulnerable while I travel.'

'I'll guard you with my life Priestess, you know that.' Culaan leant down and kissed her gently on the lips, before taking his seat back at the foot of her bed.

'Thank you.' The Priestess closed her eyes and relaxed through her breathing. Images of her old life in

Shiloh drifted to her. She smiled as she thought of her old mentor, the little Holy man who helped her overcome the barriers to astral travel. She was always so focussed on the past, or some other distracting memory to truly embrace the spirit realm.

It felt like so many years ago that she had struggled to learn the technique, but the gift came easily to her now. She felt the rush of her beating heart and the flush of warmth that preceded the calm she now relished in.

She watched the ground disappear from under her spirit body. The heat from her own body and Culaan's could be seen in her room, while Ophelia's body was otherwise occupied with the guard in the barn. The Priestess smiled at her friend's willingness to distract the guard.

Ariela focussed on the memory of Reznor's face. Her last meeting in the Goth village had been far from pleasant, but she pushed the negative thoughts from her mind.

Making contact with the conscious mind was more challenging than Ariela remembered. She came upon the village to find Reznor busy yelling orders and men running at his bidding. She reached out into his mind, but he was so distracted with his plans and emotions, she failed to reach his subconscious thoughts.

Just as she was preparing to return to her body, she saw Griffin leaning up against a post in the main clearing, calmly whittling a piece of wood with his dagger. She smiled at his relaxed manner and allowed her mind to seek out the quietness of his thoughts.

She wondered why he wasn't tracking Genevieve and Andronica but as she entered his mind, she discovered her answer. The young warrior was deep in thought, remembering where he had left Genevieve. As Ariela feared, they had not travelled far from the Senator's Estate.

Griffin had left them there to report to Reznor, but it was the lingering images of Genevieve that made Ariela feel uncomfortable about invading Griffin's thoughts. She pushed her reservations aside. The quest was too important.

'Griffin!' Ariela wrapped her hands around Griffin's face and he looked up immediately. Seeing nothing, he frowned in confusion.

'Griffin, it's Ariela.' The young warrior looked around, seeking out the source of the voice in his head.

'Ariela? Where are you?' He pushed his dagger back in its sheath and put his current project in a leather pouch at his belt.

'Long story, just listen. Andronica has convinced the Senator that the Goth village, your village is a threat. There is a full legion set to march on you at any moment. You have to warn Reznor.'

'I feel like a right fool talking to this post you know.' Griffin looked around to see if anyone was watching him. He had faced the post he had been leaning on purely so Reznor or the others wouldn't see him talking to himself.

'Just tell him. Don't fight, run. Vacate the village. We'll get there to help when we can, but we need to make sure Andronica doesn't get her hands on any more relics first.'

'Running isn't really part of Reznor's skill set.'

'A full legion Griffin. Tell him to swallow his pride and fight another day.'

'I'll do my best.'

Chapter 28

'Primus. I have it on good authority that the Goth tribes are planning an uprising.' The Senator sat in his study, staring out the window at the massing army outside.

'I find that a little hard to believe Senator, but you're in charge. What are your orders?' The Senator turned to face his Officer, who saluted and awaited his reply.

The Centurion was tall with tanned skin from years of service and eyes so dark you could barely see the pupils. His plumed helmet was tucked carefully under his arm, his short-sword strapped to his side and his cape pulled back over his shoulders.

'I think we need a show of force. I honestly don't want to have to kill any of them. They are excellent mercenaries to have on our side but they would make seriously dangerous enemies. We set an example now, before it's too late.'

'That seems a sound course of action Sir.'

'Excellent. I'll accompany you Primus. If there is any chance this is all a misunderstanding, I need to be there to find a diplomatic solution.'

'Better you than me Sir.'

The Primus saluted once more and waited for the Senator to collect his weapons and leave his study. Both men made their way down the spiral stairs and out onto the long portico that stretched the length of the stately home.

'Fetch my mount.' The Senator called to a young servant who waited patiently on the marshalling yard below the porch stairs. He scurried away hastily and returned moments later with a tall, white gelding that pranced and skipped sideways with obvious excitement.

'Efficient as always,' he smiled. 'You are a mind-reader Trent.'

The servant nodded, and bowed slightly as he handed the reigns to the Senator. 'I got him ready as soon as I saw the Primus arrive.'

'Good man. Tell Katerina I'll not be home for supper.'

'Yes Sir.' The boy bowed again and stepped forward to offer the Senator his clasped hands to help him mount. As he moved away from the Senator's gelding, he watched in awe as the Primus leapt to his stallion's back, a handful of mane his only purchase.

The Primus of the Legion smiled at the surprised look on the boy's face. 'Years of practice,' he offered and the boy could only nod in reply.

Both men pushed their mounts to a slow canter and left the main gate in a matter of moments. The cavalry had moved to await the Primus's return, but the infantry simply made an about-face and smoothly began to march to their destination. The cavalry formed up in front of them and led the way.

The vibration of so much metal and motion sent shockwaves through the ground and birds took flight from the surrounding forest.

****

Ariela opened her eyes to the sound of marching feet. She took a moment to orient herself, then smiled at Culaan, still perched and alert at the foot of her bed.

'The Legion is leaving. Did you get the message to Reznor?' Culaan moved forward to help Ariela to her feet.

'No, but I spoke with Griffin. He'll do what he can to convince Reznor to leave the village.'

'That won't be easy.'

'I know, so the quicker we secure Brísingamen, the quicker we can go and aid Reznor.'

'I'm not sure they deserve our help after what they did to you.' Culaan held Ariela in his arms a moment.

'We don't get to make those choices. He did what he thought was right. We should have been more honest to begin with. Something for us to learn from this experience.'

'We did what we thought was right at the time. Hindsight is a wonderful thing. Reznor might not deserve the help but his people do.' Culaan agreed and waved for Ariela to lead the way.

Ariela moved to the door and out into the hallway. She checked behind to make sure Culaan was following her before she moved out of the dormitory and into the cookhouse. It was a risk. If Katerina found her and raised the alarm, they might never get to Brísingamen before Andronica, but Katerina had supported her so far, so why change her mind now?

Luck was with her and she led Culaan up the shining marble stairs and into the Senator's study without incident.

'What now? Can you get into the cupboard?'

'I hope so. I saw Constantius open it without any issue.' Ariela moved to the concealed door and pushed on it. Nothing happened. She peered around the edges, looking for a hand hold or way to pull it open.

'How did Constantius do it?' Culaan asked, moving forward to see if he could assist.

'I don't know. He opened it while I wasn't exactly paying that much attention.'

'Maybe this will work?' Culaan pulled out his dagger and began to pry around the edges.

'Be careful.' Ophelia whispered intensely as she entered the study. 'It's warded by magic. It will likely have safeguards to stop theft.'

'How did Constantius open it then?' Ariela frowned as Culaan continued to pry and probe with a little more care.

'He isn't magical in any way. It's probably why the Senator and he can open the cupboard without issue.'

'And they had the key.' Ariela pointed out the obvious and Ophelia blushed with slight embarrassment.

'Well I don't have a key and I can't do any magic. Why can't *I* find a way to open it?' Culaan pushed the dagger under the lip of the door and pushed. The noise was almost deafening, but the blast of air was what really caused concern. Culaan was lifted from his legs and thrown across the room, much like Constantius was when he attacked Ariela.

'You were saying?' Ophelia raised an eyebrow as Ariela ran to check on the Celtic warrior.

'He's not magical!' Ariela insisted.

'Well, how does he wield that fancy shining sword then?'

'She's right. You remember what Morrigan said, we weren't ordinary. She didn't say we had magical ability, but she said we weren't exactly mortal either when we fought with the Druids.'

Thoughts of Morrigan made Ariela remember the relics she had in her makeshift bag.

'Katerina is going to have to have heard that noise. The guards will be here any moment.'

'The guards are the least of your issues Priestess.' Everyone spun round at the sound of Andronica's voice. She stood in the doorway, hands on hips and a smile that appeared more of a sneer on her lips.

'You'll be facing them too you know.' Ophelia challenged as she began to move further into the study, away from the entrance where she'd been standing.

'I've taken care of the staff.'

'What does that mean?' Ophelia looked from Ariela to Andronica as though considering something.

'Leave her to me Ophelia.' Ariela insisted, shaking her head at whatever Ophelia was contemplating.

'Genevieve, why don't you come and help explain what that means?' The sound of Andronica's voice seemed unusually sweet. Culaan took a step forward, but Ariela placed her hand on his arm.

'I need to speak with Genevieve,' he whispered, but Ariela shook her head and frowned.

As if answering Culaan, Genevieve moved alongside Andronica as they both made their way into the study. She looked directly at him and her features softened in a way he had never seen before. The look unnerved him and he licked his lips, looking around the room, trying to figure out how they could get the relic and escape without hurting Genevieve.

'What has she done to the guards, the servants?' Ariela directed her question at Genevieve.

'They aren't hurt... just sedated. She doesn't want to hurt anyone. We just need Brísingamen.'

Chapter 29

'What are you talking about? You've gone mad Griff.' Reznor put down his maps on the large wooden table and turned to his friend.

'No, at least I don't think so. She spoke in my head.' Griffin placed both his hands on either side of his head as though that explained everything.

'Listen to yourself.' Reznor challenged and Griffin began to reconsider his own sanity.

'Alright, humour me. Send out a scout and check to see if the Senator's men are marching on the village.' Griffin stepped forward and pulled the map closer to him. He took a cup of water and drank deeply while he studied the terrain.

'I know Ariela said to expect anything, but a full legion? That is overkill Griffin.'

'Yes, maybe, but she was adamant we shouldn't fight, that we should flee.' Griffin spun the map around as though trying to figure something out.

'And she came to you in your head?' Reznor frowned as he considered his friend.

'Yes, well sort of. I could actually feel her touch my cheeks, but her words were in my head. You said they are gods, or magical or something. I'm not here to figure out how in the name of the All-Father they managed it, but she sure was convincing.'

'Alright, you go find her Griffin and bring her to me when you do. I'll send out a scout and start moving the women and children to the caves in the hills.'

'Here! Take them here!' Griffin pushed the map toward Reznor and tapped the place he suggested. 'Expect the Legion to form up over there,' he pointed to a ravine that split the village between the higher ground where the cottages were and the lower ground where crops were grown.

'That makes sense Griff. I'll get on to it I promise, just bring Ariela and her sword-wielding friend with her. If what she says is true, I think we might need their help.'

'She said she would come as soon as she could. She's still at the Senator's Estate trying to get to the relic before Andronica does.'

'All the more reason you go help her and Culaan,' Reznor spoke the last quietly. He still hadn't told the village, especially Blaze, that Thor wasn't really Thor.

'I'll be a quick as I can.' Griffin moved toward the stables.

'Take my horse Griffin. He's the fastest. Look after him.'

'I will. But you promise me you won't stay and fight.'

'You know I can't make that promise. I'll assess the situation once the scouts return.

Griffin let out a sigh and nodded as he moved quickly to the stables.

'Genevieve. What's going on?' Culaan asked quietly as both women advanced further into the study. 'Why are you helping this woman? She's dangerous.'

'She hasn't hurt me and I told you she hasn't hurt the guards or the staff.' Genevieve offered, unconvinced by Culaan's accusations.

'But she tried to use Reznor to hurt Ariela and she has lied about the Goths to the Senator. Blaze and all the women and children in the village could be killed because of her.'

Genevieve frowned and looked at Andronica for guidance.

'No one will get hurt Genevieve. If we get Brísingamen now, before it's too late, we'll return to the past and stop all this from ever happening.'

'You can't meddle with the past Andronica.' Ariela stepped forward, placing herself protectively in front of Culaan and Ophelia.

'My name isn't Andronica. It's Andraste and I know what I'm doing. This isn't my first trip through time. I've lived hundreds of years longer than you little Priestess.'

'Andraste, where have I heard that name before?' Ariela turned to Culaan whose face showed the same confusion.

'Your old friend Morrigan may have mentioned me. We were good friends once — before she betrayed me.'

'Morrigan wouldn't betray anyone.' Ariela didn't know why she felt the need to defend the Druid.

'You only know what she told you. Owyn was a weak leader. He followed in the footsteps of his great uncle, not his great grandfather and made treaties with the Roman Empire that cost us our heritage, our magic. I tried everything to stop the Romans, but Morrigan decided I was too strong and the Druids banished me.'

'Look, I'm not exactly Owyn's greatest fan, but he's long gone now and who knows what has become of the Tolistobgii or other Galatian clans and if the Druid council banished you, I'm guessing they had good reason.' Culaan aimed his last comment at Genevieve whose brow furrowed with new found confusion.

'I know what has become of them Culaan. They were forced out of their homes by the Romans and nearly every Druid was killed. That very council that banished me are all gone, but *I'm* still here!

The Romans are no different now than they were then. I need to stop them, before they take over the Goth heritage too.'

'They no longer kill out religious cultures.' Ophelia protested and Ariela took the opportunity to reach into her bag, seeking out the relic she wanted.

'They will. The Emperor is embracing the new religion and for now he tolerates what is left of the old, but that won't last.'

'How can you open the locked door? It's warded!' Ariela changed the subject as she touched the Celtic relic and Morrigan's essence flickered, sending tingles along her fingers.

'Genevieve will open it.'

'I don't think so. Culaan couldn't.' Ariela offered.

'What are you doing?' Culaan protested quietly, but everyone could hear.

'I'm just curious.' Ariela didn't try to speak quietly, she wanted to distract Andraste.

'Culaan, don't do anything stupid, please.' Genevieve pleaded as she watched him place his hand protectively on his sword hilt.

Ariela advanced slowly, continuing to ask questions, while testing for Morrigan's power.

'You know me Genie, stupid is my middle name.' Culaan grinned.

'She's our mother!' Genevieve blurted out as Culaan's sword sprang to life in his hand.

'Whose mother?' Ariela and Culaan spoke at the same time.

'Ours, Culaan's and mine. That's what Morrigan was trying to tell us. She knew.'

'No! Lies! Just distractions by her.' Culaan pointed his sword at Andraste. '*I'm* Owyn's bastard! You're not. You can't be.'

'I am and worse. He never knew. My father was right there in the village and I never got the chance to know him, truly know him.'

Culaan looked at Genevieve and the certainty in her eyes distracted him. His sword buzzed with power as he lowered it to his side.

Ophelia moved toward the cupboard, hoping to get a chance to open it herself, while Ariela continued to advance on Andraste, her magic concealed, her eyes fixed on the Druid.

'Going back in time will have repercussions. Genevieve and Culaan may very well no longer exist. When are you returning to, before they were born, before you seduced Owyn?'

'Genevieve, open the cupboard,' Andraste pointed to Ophelia. 'and you, step away before I am forced to hurt you.'

Ophelia stopped with her hand inches away from attempting to open the door and backed away slowly.

Genevieve began to move forward. She came face to face with Ariela first, who stepped aside for her friend. 'I hope you can't open it either Genevieve or we could all be gone from the pages of history.'

'It's a small sacrifice for our people to remain free of the Roman Empire.'

'Do you really believe that going back in the past will truly change anything?' Ariela directed her question to Genevieve but Andraste answered.

'It will.'

'How can you be sure? What are you planning to do? Kill Owyn? Kill the Emperor? There are more Romans and their philosophy won't change no matter how far you go back.'

'No. I'll go back further, much further. If I can help Ortagion unite the clans, then the Roman Empire will never rise to power.'

'I wouldn't guarantee that Andraste. I'm here by the grace of God, with the power of the Angel Raziel. I'm not here to stop the Romans, I'm here to stop you. What does that tell you about your path?' Ariela directed the question to Genevieve who had reached the cupboard.

She hesitated a moment, chewing her lip, considering her friend's words. But there was something deep in the Huntress's spirit that longed to please her mother. She wanted the love of a parent she had never known before. Genevieve reached out to the locked door and felt the tingle of the magic in her hands.

She had no time to react before the bolt of power hit her in the chest. The Huntress flew from one side of the room to the other, landing hard against the bookshelves and knocking the statue of the Emperor to the ground. The sound of shattering marble caused everyone to stop and turn.

Chapter 30

Griffin dismounted. With no time to care for the lathered mount, he prayed to the goddess to keep Reznor's horse alive. He had ridden hard to make the journey as quickly as he could.

He walked through the entrance and frowned, shaking his head in confusion as he passed two guards, unconscious on the ground, their weapons still sheathed. He moved quickly, but carefully up the front steps of the stately home. The marble portico shone in the sun, reflecting light in a way that left bright spots before the warrior's eyes.

He gently pushed the heavy double doors open to discover a rounded middle-aged woman laying sprawled on the thickly woven carpet that covered the stone floor of the foyer. Griffin stepped quietly past her, checking her for signs of life. She was breathing, but there was no sign of injury.

He could hear voices up the spiral staircase and the crashing sound that reverberated down set his heart racing. He took the stairs two at time, thankful that with all the commotion above, he was able to advance quickly and remain unheard.

'Are you alright Genie?' he heard Culaan ask.

Griffin was torn between aiding the Huntress or staying unseen. If he barged in, the Healer would likely do to him, whatever she had done to all the guards below, but if he did nothing, he knew Ariela and her friends would be in danger.

He drew his sword and peeked around the corner of the doorway. Genevieve was struggling for consciousness on the floor. Culaan was on one knee by her side. He could see Ariela over the shoulder of the Healer who still had her back to him.

'I told you Genevieve would not be able to open the cupboard. None of us can. It's warded. Only a mortal can open it.' Ariela had seen him he knew and she was speaking to him, even if she wasn't looking at him. *Was he the only mortal in the room? Could he open the cupboard? What did he need to do, leave so he wouldn't be able to open it or hide and open it when he got the chance?*

His decision was taken from him when the Healer turned to look straight at him. 'Your use of the word mortal was a little obvious Ariela.' Andraste pointed straight at Griffin. '*You* can open the cupboard and give me the relic.'

He looked from the Healer to Ariela who shook her head, unseen by the fierce looking woman before him. He tried to move backwards out of the room, but it was too late. He had lost control of his own limbs. His hand rose and placed his sword back into the sheath at his hip before he began walking to a bookcase behind the Senator's desk.

'Griffin, what are you doing?' Ariela begged him to stop.

He could barely control his eyebrows, which rose with an unmistakable look of fear. His hand was raising towards a wooden door that sat between rows of multi-coloured scrolls and ornaments. His hand shook with the effort of control, but no matter how hard he tried, his hand did not obey him.

Genevieve watched as Griffin was forced to do her mother's bidding. 'Mother, stop!'

'Genevieve, you will thank me when we are done.' Andraste remained focussed on the young warrior.

'No! Stop! Griffin is not our puppet to control. He is one of the very people you claim to be protecting.'

'I thought you were different child. I thought your life would have hardened you enough to not be weak when I really needed you.'

'She isn't weak! She is one of the strongest and most honourable women I've ever known.' Culaan helped Genevieve to her feet as he spoke and they exchanged a look that they both knew well.

The door to the cupboard opened and Griffin reached in for Brísingamen. It glowed with power and both Andraste and Ariela gasped as the essence of the relic filled the room.

'Bring it to me.' Andraste demanded and Griffin began walking towards the Healer, Brísingamen balanced over the palm of his hand. It was designed as a necklace, to encircle the wearer. The clasp was open, ready to be placed on the neck of the magic wielder.

The open ends of the clasp swayed either side of Griffin's hand, mesmerising and tempting with its promise of power.

Genevieve and Culaan moved to surround Griffin, one either side. 'I'm sorry,' was all Genevieve said to Griffin before she barged into his body, sending him sprawling to the floor. Culaan moved in on the Goth warrior quickly, forcing his body to the ground with his foot.

Brísingamen flew free of his grip as he landed hard and both Ariela and Andraste moved toward it, trying to pluck if from the air.

'I'm good guys. You can let me go now.' Griffin finally spoke, free of Andraste's hold as she fought to reach Brísingamen before the Priestess.

All three warriors sprang to their feet. Culaan and Griffin drew their swords, while Genevieve pulled her ever present bow from her shoulder, before realising the close quarters were no place for such a weapon. She looked at Ophelia who had squeezed herself into the corner of the study, trying to become invisible and pointed to the statue that stood on a pedestal beside the window.

The Guardian looked and nodded, and lifting the heavy object, she used all her effort to throw it to the Huntress.

Andraste reached Brísingamen first, clasping it in her hand like her life depended on it. Ariela stepped back once she realised she had missed the relic and returned her hand to the one in her bag.

Andraste lifted Brísingamen to her neck and clipped the clasp closed. Her face began to glow like a golden statue and a ring of light circled her body. Ariela knew she didn't have long before the Druid would leave this time and alter history forever.

She pulled the three-pointed Celtic star from the bag and prayed she was right. Next, she reached for her mother's talisman. With both relics exposed, Andraste suddenly looked panicked and began chanting in a language Ariela had never heard.

The Priestess held her hands out in front of her, one relic in each. She had no idea how to draw on the power, but she knew one was once Morrigan's and the other had been her mother's. Having known both women, gave her the advantage she needed.

She thought of them in her heart which ached for the loss of them. She closed her eyes and drew on the power she felt welling up inside her chest. When she opened her eyes, her entire body was glowing with a blue light and her feet were no longer on the ground.

Andraste's entire body too was alight with the brightness of the sun and Ariela felt panic for the first time. She opened her palms to the Druid before her. The relics did not fall from her hands, instead they fired a burst of power so strong it threw both women in opposite directions.

Culaan watched Ariela hit the wall and realised she wasn't going to regain consciousness immediately. He quickly swung to Andraste to find she was in the same condition.

Genevieve beat him to the Druid. She unclipped Brísingamen, handing it to Ophelia who had moved up behind the Huntress. Ophelia rushed over to Ariela and placed Brísingamen around her neck, clasping it quickly in place.

'What did you do that for?' Culaan looked from Andraste to Ariela confused.

'Ariela can bind her. We just need to hope she wakes up first.' Ophelia bent down and began gently tapping Ariela on the face. 'Wake up Ariela… please wake up.'

Andraste began to stir, but Genevieve and Griffin had her on her face, her hands were being tied behind her back with a leather rope.

'I'm sorry Culaan. I don't know what came over me.' Genevieve begged for her brother's forgiveness.

'I get it Genie. I do. I always wanted to know who my mother was. It's just a shame she turned out to be stark raving mad.' The boyish grin returned to his face without missing a beat and Genevieve laughed aloud.

'She had me convinced.' Genevieve's smile faded.

'She had me scared witless.' Griffin offered.

'You have no idea boy.' Griffin leapt to his feet reflexively as the Druid spoke.

Genevieve added her weight to the Healer's back, trying to keep her from making eye contact or using any part of her body to call on her magic. 'Is Ariela awake?' She looked expectantly across the room to Culaan and Ophelia.

Ophelia nodded and smiled as Ariela pushed herself to her feet, aided by Culaan and the Guardian.

'I have no idea how to use this,' she whispered to Ophelia.

'The Angel is with you Priestess. Do what you need to do.'

Ariela reached for the two relics that were on the ground either side of her. As soon as they were both in her hands, she felt a surge of energy so unfamiliar that it almost made her faint.

'Don't go flitting through time without me Ariela.' Culaan warned.

'I'll try not to.' She smiled reassuringly before she closed her eyes and focussed on Brísingamen. It was speaking to her, not in words, but in images. She saw the Roman's marching on Reznor's village. She saw Constantius setting a pyre alight, a woman tied to a stake screaming into the night. It wasn't the Constantius she knew. He was an older version of himself, more hardened. The vision made her shudder.

'We have to hurry. Reznor needs us.' Ariela spoke through her vision.

'We are only waiting on you.' Culaan risked touching her for reassurance. The combined energy of the warrior surged through Ariela like liquid fire, the resulting force drew on the Druid before them.

Andraste screamed and writhed on the ground. 'No! No! You can't have my power!'

Culaan looked at his mother squirming below Genevieve and realisation struck. 'Genevieve, leave her with Griffin and come here.'

Griffin looked dubiously at Culaan and Genevieve before finally taking the Huntress's place — his knee on the woman's back so she couldn't rise.

'Culaan, we need to move quickly.' Ariela begged through clenched teeth.

'Genevieve, touch Ariela.' The Huntress looked confused but Culaan nodded at his own hand on Ariela's shoulder and Genevieve mimicked him on the Priestess's other shoulder.

The pull of energy forced Ariela's chest forward and her back arched. Her feet left the ground once more and a bright green and blue light surrounded her and the two warriors by her side.

Culaan and Genevieve held her in place, but their bodies were vibrating as all three felt the power of the Druid before them. The surge lasted only a few heartbeats but the result left all three tingling with the sensation.

'What just happened?' Genevieve took a deep breath, fighting for air. Her whole body shuddered with a mixture of pain and euphoria.

'I think you just got your inheritance.' Ariela smiled before she collapsed to the ground.

'Are you alright?' Culaan dropped to his knees, cradling Ariela in his arms. He kissed her cheek and the Priestess smiled at his touch.

'I'll be fine. I just need a moment. We have to get to Reznor and stop the Senator. Reznor evacuated all the women and children, but he has kept all his warriors in the village.'

'Why doesn't that surprise me?' Culaan looked at Griffin, who smiled his understanding, his knee still placed firmly in the Druid's back.

Chapter 31

Reznor stood in the middle of the gully Griffin had pointed out. He had been right. The Legion had arrived not long after he left.

None of this made any sense. Why would the Romans attack his people? Ariela had warned him, but he hadn't expected a full legion, maybe a vanguard of cavalry or some foot soldiers, but a Legion? It was overkill.

He only had five hundred men at his immediate disposal. Maybe that was the point. Take him and his main force out quickly and then attack the remaining village communities, but why?

The Senator rode forward with the Primus of the Centurions' forces at his side, but it was the younger noble who accompanied him that had Reznor ill at ease.

'Reznor. What is this?' The Senator waved his hand at the wall of men that stood at the Goth leader's back.

'We heard you were coming. Thought we would bring out the welcoming party.' Reznor curved his lips, but it wasn't a smile.

'We heard something similar.'

'It seems we might have both been misled.' Reznor searched the Senator's face for any sign of deceit, but there was none.

'Andronica has been acting very strangely of late,' Reznor offered as some form of explanation.

'She isn't the only one. Can I introduce the Emperor's son, Constantius? Constantius, this is our friend and ally Reznor. He won't say it but he basically rules all the Goth tribes of this region.'

'So I have been told.' Constantius pushed his mount forward so that he was side by side with the Senator. No one saw the weapon reach his hand, but the uproar that followed it entering the Senator's chest, just below his left arm was instant.

Reznor backed his horse up but the animal was slow to react. His own mount would have moved instinctively with his rider. Constantius's sword swung by Reznor's cheek and a small cut appeared above his cheek bone.

'What kind of peace meeting is this?' Reznor roared.

'You heard the Senator.' Constantius calmly looked at the man choking on his own blood next to him, without regard. 'I'm the son of the Emperor. *I'm* in charge and I see no need to make peace with men who use magic to control others.'

'What are you talking about?' Reznor wiped the blood from his cheek and looked at his men, nodding to his second to make ready for war.

'You sent Andronica to me to drug me and steal from me. Now Primus, I believe I am the next in charge, is that correct?' Constantius spoke without looking at the man, his eyes fixed on Reznor.

The Primus pursed his lips for only a moment before saluting his new, self-appointed leader. 'It would seem that you are my lord.' The Primus bowed his head and backed his horse up a few paces. 'What are your orders?'

'Kill them all.' Constantius demanded as he rounded his mount and cantered from the field.

****

'We don't have much time. Bring her with you.' Ariela pointed to Andraste who lay weeping on the ground, now posing no threat, she had been allowed to sit up, her hands still tied behind her back.

'It will take at least an hour to get to the village with this many people.' Griffin protested. 'We'll be too late.'

'I have an idea.' Ariela tucked her mother's relic under her arm and pushed the other into her bag. She wasn't sure if what she wanted to do was possible, but for now she didn't remove Brísingamen from around her neck.

'Gather around me, hold hands with the person next to you. Ophelia and Griffin, you keep Andraste between the two of you. I'm not sure I've locked off her power yet. I don't want her getting too close to either of you.' She looked at Genevieve and Culaan and they both nodded.

Ariela stepped forward and pulled the amulet from Andraste's neck, she placed it in her bag. She then spun the Druid around and pried the bone ring from her hand. 'Just in case.' She stared at the Druid who snarled quietly at the last relic of magic being taken from her.

'Close your eyes. This might get bright.' Ariela stepped back and took Culaan and Genevieve by the hand.

'What are you doing Ariela?' Culaan sounded a little sceptical.

'I'm trying my hand at travelling… not through time, just space.'

'I'm guessing you have never done this before?'

'You're guessing right.'

'Do we all have to be your test subjects?' Griffin asked just as the ground below their feet began to vibrate. 'Oh god no! Please don't let me die.'

'Who are you praying to?' Genevieve smiled at his discomfort. This wasn't entirely new to her.

'Anyone who is listening.' Griffin answered as he unashamedly scrunched his eyes closed and squeezed Genevieve's hand.

Culaan exchanged glances with Genevieve who shrugged. The world went dark, before a burst of light, brighter than the sunniest day, left anyone with their eyes still open sun blinded.

'Did it work?' Griffin asked, his eyes still closed tightly. Ophelia slapped him on the shoulder as the sound of steel on steel reached them.

'What now?' Ophelia looked to Culaan as he drew his sword and Genevieve notched a bolt to her bow.

'Now we prove to the Senator that Andraste was lying to him.' Ariela grabbed the impotent Druid and pushed her in front as they moved toward the sound of fighting.

They came through the back of the village from behind Andraste's cottage to see the village overrun with soldiers. Reznor held a defensive line across the middle of the village square and Ariela nearly cried out as she saw Constantius sitting comfortably on his horse a few hundred paces from the battle on a slight rise.

'What is he doing here?' Culaan asked the question Ariela had already been thinking.

'I have no idea, but I had a vision and if he is here, it might have been a prophecy and not a good one.'

'Do we kill him then?' Culaan asked a little too eagerly.

'I don't think so Culaan, but I honestly don't know.'

'Let's help Reznor while we still can. Do you think you can dissuade Constantius without more bloodshed?'

'I hope so.'

'Genie, you and I will reinforce Reznor. Griffin, you can join us.' Culaan moved forward to join the fight.

'Ophelia, take her somewhere safe, but not too far away. Constantius is unstable because of her. If we can prove we have her under control, I might be able to fix this for now.' Ophelia nodded as Ariela moved away.

Chapter 32

'About time you got here Griff. Where's my horse?' Reznor didn't take his eyes off the battle before him as Griffin pulled a chain-mail shirt on over his head and stepped forward to join his leader.

'Sorry. We couldn't exactly bring him with us.' The young warrior intercepted a sword blow just before it reached Reznor's head and both men smiled at one another.

'We'll explain later. We need to give Ariela a little time.' Culaan moved alongside the leader, his sword glowing menacingly. A fired arrow flew past his head, taking a Roman soldier in the chest. His mail shirt had offered no protection against the magical weapon. Culaan risked a glance to check on Genevieve's location. She always managed to find the best vantage point for her weapon.

He spotted her high in the old oak tree that stood in the centre of the village square.

'She's deadly with that thing.' Griffin whistled as another bolt landed and took another soldier in the neck.

'She's just deadly, with or without a weapon. Best you remember that, in case you have any ideas.' Culaan warned, as he fended off another soldier and struck him in the chest with his weapon, which passed cleanly through the bronze shield and armour. The life left his eyes instantly, for which Culaan was thankful. None of these men deserved to die today.

'She was coming on to me and you know it.' Griffin protested.

'Have it your way.' Culaan grinned and Griffin ducked under an arched sword swing that narrowly missed his neck and slid off the mail shirt he had just hastily put on.

****

Constantius watched the battle. It was amazing. The thrill of leadership pulsed through his veins as he sat with the Primus, deciding on the next course of action.

'When do you suggest we use the cavalry Primus?'

'The village isn't big enough for a full force frontal attack my lord. I'd suggest we use the cavalry to mop up the stragglers when they rout.'

'The Goths aren't known for routing Primus.' Constantius rubbed his chin as he saw the magical warriors join the field. 'We have to stamp out that magic.'

The Primus followed Constantius's line of sight and saw Culaan's glowing sword enter the line. 'How do we do that my Lord?'

Constantius saw Ariela and his stomach did a summersault. When he had left Ariela he had felt a sudden and overwhelming sense of melancholy pushing him down once again. He had returned to his room and found the last of the herbs that the Healer had given him.

His mind had told him he shouldn't take it, but his body craved it more than it craved the warmth of a woman's body, more than air itself.

Now, the herbs ran through his body and set all his senses on fire. The mere sight of Ariela fired him inside and out. He wanted her and for him to have her, he needed to end the warrior with the pretty glowing sword.

'Primus, throw all your men at that one warrior. He can't leave this field alive.' The Centurion saluted and moved to give the order. 'And Primus, I'll have that weapon when you're finished.'

The Primus moved away toward the Optio, second in command of his infantry, and gave the order. It held no joy for him. He'd fought alongside Reznor on numerous occasions. The man was all honour and courage. This day was not likely to end well for anyone.

The infantry men heard the Hastati spear cohort moving forward in tight formation, each step firmly placed and loud enough to fill the enemy with dread. Over two hundred men stomping their feet in perfect, synchronised motion was enough to make the ground vibrate.

The Primus saw the glowing arrows raining down from the tree in the centre of the village, but his Hastati held their shields aloft, not one arrow penetrated the metal.

He was so focussed on the field of battle below, he failed to see the woman approach from the forest behind them.

'Constantius! Stop this! *Please!*' Ariela pleaded
with the new Roman Lord. The Primus remained where
he was, awaiting his new Lord's orders, watching the
small woman approach without fear.

'You are just another witch, just like them.'
Constantius pointed down in the village at her friends.

'No! *She* was the witch.' Ariela pointed to
Andraste, who was being pushed forward by Ophelia,
who remained shielded by the Druid's body. 'She
drugged you.' The Priestess looked at the dark rings
around Constantius's eyes and anger rose in her heart.
'and it seems made you dependent on that drug. She is
the one who deceived the Senator, deceived you. She has
no power anymore Constantius. It's gone.'

The Emperor's son shook his head, the fog of the
drug still making his mind feel like it was clawing
through thick mud. It didn't matter now, he had killed
the Senator and his father would be angry, not
disappointed in him. He was always a disappointment to
his father.

'Constantius, please! Call off the soldiers. These
people did nothing wrong. Andronica lied to you.'

'No, she just proved to me that the Goths have
magic that the Roman Empire cannot afford to ignore.'

'There is magic everywhere, even the new religion
your father follows has magic in it. Leave these people,
ask you father about the magic of the Prophet, about the
new religion.'

'No, if that is the truth, then the new religion must
have the most powerful magic. I need to stamp out the
Goth magic now.'

Ariela moved closer to the Noble and thankfully the Centurion didn't seem to see her as a threat. 'If you believe in the new religion, then you must believe its magic will do the work for you. You must trust it. You don't need to kill these people.'

Ariela looked down on the village and could see the fighting escalating. She didn't want to lose Culaan, or Genevieve. Something happened in that moment. She was unsure what she was really there for. To stop Andraste or Constantius?

If it was to stop Andraste, why hadn't the Angel come to take them away yet? Something was unresolved. It was likely just this fight, but how was she going to stop Constantius and restore peace between the Romans and the Goths?

Ariela chanced a look at the Primus who had still not moved to stop her. A thought suddenly dawned on her. He wanted her to stop Constantius but he couldn't do it himself. As if her thoughts could be heard by the Soldier, he nodded gently to her and she understood what she needed to do.

Ariela drew energy from the air around her. She didn't need Brísingamen for this, but she did hold her mother's amulet. She could feel her mother in every touch. The strength, the compassion, the love seeped into her spirit.

Chapter 33

Genevieve had seen enough. Her weapon was useless against the shield wall of spear carrying warriors. They left no opening as they drew closer with every loud vibrating stomp of their feet.

She shouldered her bow and shimmied down the tree. She pulled a short-sword from a dead soldier as she strode purposefully across the town square to join the front line with Culaan and Griffin.

'Make room for a lady boys.' Genevieve moved between the two men.

'You're clogging up my sword arm you know.' Culaan smiled at his sister. 'It's not going to be quite the same now, between you and me.'

The siblings made idle chatter to calm their nerves as the shield wall advanced slowly. 'What, because I'm your sister? I'm just so glad I never convinced you to sleep with me.'

Griffin nearly choked on his own spittle next to her and she looked at him like he had two heads. 'What are you so shocked about? I know, can you believe he refused me more times than I can remember? I didn't know he was my brother then though.'

'What are you more upset about, he refused you, or he was your brother?'

'That he refused me of course.'

The conversation ceased as the spearmen reached their destination. The shield wall didn't even open, but the long wooden spears appeared like magic, thrusting and stabbing at whatever was in front of them. Warriors cried out and were pulled clear so fresh fighters could take their place.

Culaan's sword swung down with little effort, cutting the end of the spears and making them smoulder as though they'd been through a forest fire. The warrior smiled and Genevieve suddenly realised what he was thinking. She threw the sword to the side and retrieved her bow from her shoulder.

'Give me a little room Griffin. I think I can set a few of these boys on fire from here.'

Griffin moved aside slightly but as Genevieve was just about to draw her bow, a spear thrust came forward without warning. Genevieve shot into the tiny opening, setting the wielder on fire, but as she drew the next bolt, she saw that the spear had found a target.

Griffin clutched his chest; his hands were covered in his own blood and his eyes grew wide with shock. Genevieve shouldered her bow and dropped to the ground, pulling the Goth warrior away from the front line, but not before noticing her fire hadn't only hit her mark, it was now rippling through the entire line of spearmen.

****

Ariela released the energy she had drawn to her. The air blast hit Constantius full in the chest and knocked him from his mount. He landed hard but not hard enough to knock him out entirely.

The Primus moved to support the Emperor's son. He had no choice. If he was seen doing nothing, he would suffer the consequences later. Ariela pushed at him with her open palm, sending him sliding backwards, his heels leaving deep tracks in the dirt.

With one hand holding back the Primus, she ran to Constantius. His horse leapt away from her and galloped into the forest, leaving its rider abandoned on the ground.

Constantius rolled to all fours and jumped to his feet. He looked at the Centurion, trapped behind Ariela's wall of power and called to any soldier who was within hearing.

'You leave me no choice Constantius. I won't kill you, but just remember, it was not Goth magic that did this to you, it was the magic of the Angels, the heavenly Angels that saw fit to stop your madness.'

The dirt took flight, the leaves from the forest floor flew into the air like sharp knives. They circled the future Emperor and cut him off from the world around him, only Ariela could be seen inside the swirling air of debris.

Ariela caught sight of Ophelia and Andraste, but it was too late. The woman managed to overpower the Guardian but the Priestess had to save her friends, had to stop the fighting and taking Constantius from this place was the only way.

****

When the debris settled, the Primus looked around. The noble brat and the woman of magic were gone. That was a blessing in disguise, he only hoped the boy wasn't dead, because that might mean his commission was over; unless he came up with the right story of course.

The Primus called his second over and the horn sounded a few moments later. The infantry moved in to create a shield wall in front of the village warriors. One line in front with shields held tightly, the second row, held their shields aloft to protect the first from archers.

The sound of thundering footsteps away from the battle confused the Goth warriors, until they looked up to see the Hastati retreating.

****

Genevieve held Griffin in her arms, a few paces behind the tightly-held Goth line. She had no idea what was happening. She couldn't explain exactly why but the sight of Griffin holding his chest, with blood oozing from between his fingers had broken through a wall she didn't know she had erected.

'You'll be alright you know.' She smiled as the tears rolled down her cheeks. 'I really like you. You know that don't you?' The tears continued and as Genevieve looked down, she could see that Griffin had stopped seeing anything. He wouldn't ever see anything again.

The rage was deep down. It didn't erupt like the volcano of power that usually signalled the Huntress's emotional state. There was something else this time, a humming like the sound of bees, but she could feel it in her soul.

I'll take care of him Huntress. She looked up and saw no one talking to her, only the back of the warrior line, in front of a wall of shields that hadn't been there a moment before.

He won't come until you let him Genevieve. Tell him it is alright… he can leave. Genevieve stroked Griffin's unshaven cheeks and kissed his forehead. 'I'm sorry we didn't have more time. But it's time to go Griffin. I don't know this Angel, but I've met one before. He'll look after you.'

Genevieve didn't see Griffin's spirit leave, but she felt it. The humming in her soul ceased and she cried like she had never cried in her life. Time stood still until Culaan's hand appeared on her shoulder. She lifted her shoulder to her cheek and felt the warmth of her brother's hand, offering her comfort.

'It's over Genie. They've all gone.'

The Huntress nodded, not really understanding what was being said to her.

'Can you look after her Reznor? I have to go find Ariela?'

'I'll look after both of them.'

Culaan nodded. 'I'm sorry.'

'You and me both.' Reznor bent down and waved a few more warriors over to him as he spoke softly to Genevieve who would not let go of the still form in her arms.

Chapter 34

A few hours passed and Culaan had not seen
Ariela. He had found Ophelia unconscious near the
forest where the Roman soldiers had congregated.
Constantius was gone and that left an uneasy feeling in
the pit of his stomach.

'There were no tracks.' Culaan complained after
getting Ophelia back to the village.

'The last I saw, Ariela was calling on her magic to
create a spiral-like void. There was debris flying
everywhere. Leaves, dirt, sticks, everything. Andraste
knocked me out. I guess she ran.'

'Did she make it to Ariela or did she escape a
different way?' Culaan was pacing as Ophelia rubbed her
temples and sipped at cup of water. They sat on a
partially broken wooden bench in the village. There were
people working to clear the mess away, but the only
place to lay the dead was on the grass below the tall trees
in the village square.

Culaan had seen worse, but Ophelia had never
seen anything like it. She wavered from nausea to grief as
the warrior before her frantically tried to assess where
the Priestess had gone.

'She was making another travel tunnel. It sounds more like what the Angel creates when we move through time though. Did she have Brísingamen on?'

'I don't think so. She wouldn't go back in time after everything we talked about. Would she? It's too dangerous.'

The sound of hooves came to them and Culaan looked up to see a robed figure riding into the village. He didn't need to see her face to know it was Ariela. He ran to meet her as she reined in her mount and dismounted.

Her feet didn't reach the ground. She was in his arms, her lips smothered with his before a word could be uttered.

'I thought I'd lost you again. You have to stop doing this to me.'

'I had to get Constantius away. Did the Primus stop the fighting?'

'He did. He spoke to Reznor, apologised, collect his injured and dead and left like it was just a routine training manoeuvre. It was plain old weird.'

'He didn't want to fight. I could see it in his eyes. It was Constantius who wanted it.'

'Andraste escaped.' Culaan wrapped his arm around Ariela's shoulder and walked her toward Ophelia. 'Brace yourself, there are so many dead.'

'I wish I could have stopped him faster.'

'Are you kidding, you did everything you could. What did you do with Constantius?'

'He was so wrapped up in our magic. His belief that Celtic and Goth magic was evil was eating at his soul. I found a group of rabbis of the new religion who took him in. They are a community that abstains from politics, and the worldly powers that be. Maybe they can work some sense into his mind. They will send word to his father. He needs to be cleaned of that foul drug Andraste gave him. You should have seen him Culaan. He had taken it again, even after knowing what it would do to him. I don't understand why?'

'I can't say for sure, but he never seemed like he was a happy person. Being the son of the Lord of the Land can have severe disadvantages and he isn't a warrior in the true sense. Maybe the drug made him feel strong.'

'Maybe you are right. I hope they can help him.'

'Do we find Andraste before we go?'

'I don't think so. I think we are done with her. I can feel Raziel now, he is close.'

'We had best get Genevieve then.'

Ophelia had heard the end of their conversation as they sat down near her. 'Can I come with you? You have all the relics now. There is nothing left for me to guard, not in this time anyway.'

Ariela looked at Culaan who smiled. 'Another woman, I'll be in my element you know.'

Ophelia and Ariela rolled their eyes. 'We could bring Griffin along.' Ariela offered. 'I think Genevieve would like that; she's rather partial to him.'

Both of her friends frowned and Ariela knew something was wrong straight away. 'We lost him Ariela. A spear in the chest. Genie has taken it very hard.'

'I didn't know. I need to find her. We have to go soon and I know it's terrible timing, but we won't be able to say goodbye properly.'

****

Genevieve laid out Griffin's body and stood over him for some time, praying to anyone who might listen.

'He was a good man.' Reznor came alongside the Huntress and touched her shoulder. 'He liked you, a lot.'

'I know. I liked him too.' Genevieve's tears were all gone now. She had never let her emotions get the better of her like she had when Griffin had died in her arms. It was everything that had happened lately. Being reunited with her mother only to discover she was an insane control freak had taken its toll.

'He didn't have any family. I think it's good that someone will miss him, not just me.'

Genevieve turned to Reznor and searched his face. 'I had no idea. No wonder we got along so well; we were both orphans.'

'Not anymore. You had each other for only a little time, but you shared something that no one can take away from you.' Reznor touched her arm and smiled before walking away to leave her with her thoughts.

Genevieve recalled the voice in her head and wondered if she had imagined it, but even if she had, she felt better believing Griffin was in a safe place.

'Are you doing alright?' Ariela wrapped her arm around her friend. 'I'm so sorry. I really liked him too.'

'Did you hear Andraste got away?'

'I did.' Ariela allowed her friend to change the subject even though her eyes were still transfixed on the body wrapped in a shroud on the ground before her.

'Do we need to kill her?'

'We don't, but we do need to leave, very soon.'

'I had thought of staying, until Griffin died. Now…' She left the words unsaid.

'Now we start another new journey. We meet more amazing people like Griffin and we fight more looney ones like your mother.' Ariela smiled and Genevieve retuned it with genuine warmth.

'We can't stay long enough, can we?' Genevieve asked, knowing the answer.

'We have to go soon. Is Griffin's family here? Can we do the ceremony before we go?'

'He has no family, except Reznor.'

Ariela had a sudden thought and before she realised, she was sending a message across the ethereal to Culaan and Reznor.

'I have an idea. I think the Angel can wait a few more minutes.' Genevieve was about to ask more when Culaan arrived with Ophelia, Reznor only a few moments behind them.

'What!' Genevieve finally voiced.

'We will have a ceremony earlier than the rest.' Reznor, and a few of Griffin's fellow warriors walked into the clearing and lifted Griffin's shrouded body up in one smooth motion. Blaze followed his father and the funeral procession began. Genevieve, Culaan, Ariela and Ophelia walked together down toward the Healer's cottage and to the clearing beyond.

It only took a moment for everyone to collect up a small amount of firewood each and build a pyre. There was no need for fire, Genevieve drew an arrow that sizzled with white fire and shot the bolt into the shrouded body.

There were no tears, as Culaan began to sing an old Celtic song of warriors and heroes. The Goths didn't speak the language but that didn't seem to matter to them. They understood without words.

The fire died down and the wind picked up speed. Reznor looked questioningly at Culaan. 'The Angel comes for us. Time to go.'

'Who are you really?'

'We told you. We were sent by the gods. We fly on the wings of Angels.' Culaan smiled as the brightest of lights filled the clearing.

We have a new friend Raziel. Ariela didn't ask for permission. She knew the Angel would oblige.

'Brace yourself Ophelia, this isn't as pleasant as you might be hoping. Hold my hand and don't let go, whatever you do.'

What Now?

If you enjoyed *Relic Seeker*, I would really love to hear from you. You can leave a review with your favourite e-book retailer.

While you are waiting for the next instalment in *The Priestess Chronicles* series, why not download the first book in my complete first series, absolutely free. You will find it on my website www.atime2write.com.au

Dedication

This book is dedicated to anyone who has ever sacrificed their own wants and needs for the good of others and done so without expectation of a reward in this life or the next. You are a rare and precious find.

Thanks to my beta team George and Rachel. Your feedback is always awesome and helps to shape each and every story. Thanks to my cover designer Simon and my editor Adele. Love your work, both of you!

Books by Fiona Tarr

Covenant of Grace Series
Destiny of Kings
Seed of Hope
Legacy of Power
Heir of Vengeance
The Ehud Dagger Novella
The Complete Collection – all 5 books

****

The Eternal Realm Series
The Jericho Prophecy
Delilah and the Dark God
Reign of Retribution

****

The Priestess Chronicles
Call of the Druids
Relic Seeker

****

All books are available from your preferred book retailer or you can find the links on my website www.atime2write.com.au. I enjoy hearing from you, so please check out the free newsletter sign up on my website and enjoy pre-release offers and more.

www.ingramcontent.com/pod-product-compliance
Lightning Source LLC
Chambersburg PA
CBHW070320120726

47909CB00008B/2523